JEff COOPER

THE FINAL ACCOUNT

The Final Account
A Jack Collins Thriller
Red Adept Publishing, LLC
104 Bugenfield Court
Garner, NC 27529
https://RedAdeptPublishing.com/
Copyright © 2025 by Jeff Cooper. All rights reserved.

Cover Art by Streetlight Graphics[1]

This is a work of fiction. Names, characters, places, and incidents either are the product of the author's imagination or are used fictitiously, and any resemblance to locales, events, business establishments, or actual persons—living or dead—is entirely coincidental.

---

1.   http://StreetlightGraphics.com

To Benjamin, Ethan, and Colleen

Chapter 1

Tom Nelson stepped into the room and approached the bed, where a plain white sheet covered Samuel Heller's lifeless body. He scanned the length of the pristine fabric as he thought of the figure lying beneath. His eyes misted as he reflected on the finality of death. *At least your suffering is over. Mine, apparently, continues on.*

Tom turned his attention to the man standing on the other side of the massive bedroom. Despite the early hour, Kyle Stone was his usual model of precision. His uniform was perfectly pressed, the brass buttons gleaming in the early-morning light. His brown hair looked as if it had just been trimmed, the top slightly thinner and spikier than the tightly groomed sides. A clean-shaven face revealed not a hint of emotion, his notorious steadiness maintained even in the presence of fresh death.

"I didn't expect you to be here," Tom said.

"Where did you think I called you from?" Kyle asked.

"That's not what I meant. I knew you were here. I just meant *why?*"

"I was in the neighborhood."

"On a Sunday morning?" Tom asked, his stomach clenching.

"Don't ask stupid questions."

Tom decided to change the subject, at least for now. "Anyone else here?"

Kyle waved his hand toward the bedroom door. "His wife's somewhere. She's with her nurse."

"Is Mrs. Heller doing all right?"

"Yeah, she's fine. She has no clue what the hell is going on. She's lucky she's losing her marbles." After an awkward chuckle, he added, "You know what I mean."

1

Tom knew all too well. He'd seen his own mother slip off into that void, unable to recognize her own friends and family long before she died.

Breaking away from Kyle's glare, Tom walked across the room until he reached an ornate walnut dresser. Lifting the framed wedding photo off the top, he stared at the youthful faces. "Nearly sixty years these two were married," he said. "That's a hell of a long time."

"Sure is."

Sixty years. Six long decades. As long as he'd been alive. In many ways, Sam and Sarah Heller had been destined for such a lasting journey together. Their fathers had once been business partners operating one of Europe's finest clothing stores. But then came hatred and violence, soon followed by war. Fortunately, both men had the means to make their way off a troubled continent and begin new lives, one settling in New York and the other moving to Chicago. They each restarted what would be wildly successful careers. Marriages and births ensued. And though the two men lost touch, fate later brought their offspring, Sam and Sarah, together on the same college campus.

While luck had drawn the Hellers into each other's arms, it had not been their constant companion. One daughter had died in childbirth, the other in childhood. Their only son had left home at eighteen and rarely returned, rejecting the trappings of Greenwich in favor of a simple life on a rural Vermont farm.

Kyle's voice interrupted Tom's silent reflection. "You ready to do your part?"

Tom swallowed hard. He was so sick of the whole operation. He'd tried to get out at every turn, begging for his freedom every time that Kyle came calling. Finally, a year ago, Kyle had seemingly relented and cut him loose, leaving him free to make a fresh start as he neared retirement.

But the freedom hadn't lasted. They called him back in, dangling the old threats and debts in front of him once again. They said Sam

Heller had incurable cancer. His demented wife had no real understanding of the scope of their wealth. It had been too big an opportunity to let pass by, too sophisticated a con to pull off without Tom's access. So he found himself in the middle yet again. *One final time*, Kyle had promised, just as he'd done before. Tom didn't believe him anymore.

"Yes, I'm all set," Tom replied with no enthusiasm. "I know what I need to do." He'd been through the routine more times than he cared to remember.

Tom replaced the photo on the dresser. His thoughts turned from the money to a more mundane task ahead of him as executor of the estate: cleaning out Heller's lifetime of accumulated belongings.

He slid open the top drawer of the dresser to get a sense of what lay ahead. After rummaging through some empty prescription bottles and unopened mail, he happened upon a wooden box tucked in the back corner. He lifted the lid and sifted through a small pile of cufflinks and spare change. Something nestled at the bottom caught his eye.

He lifted the watch out of the box and cupped it in his hand. The black leather straps dangled between his fingers. The square gold body felt cold against his palm. He raised the watch and squinted at the black lettering on the yellow face. His heart began to flutter. *Lange? A prewar Lange? Seriously?*

"Let me have a look," Kyle demanded.

Tom hesitated.

"Now," Kyle ordered.

Tom walked over and surrendered the timepiece to Kyle's outstretched hand. The watch soon disappeared into the man's pocket.

"We shouldn't," Tom said. "That should stay."

"I want this one. You can have the next one."

"That's not the point. That watch is unique. It was probably—"

"Enough," Kyle snapped. "Now, I should get moving."

"Anyone call the funeral home?" Tom asked meekly.

"No, you need to do all that. And get that nurse on the first flight back to Poland."

"Slovakia."

"Wherever. Just get rid of her."

Tom nodded. "I'll take care of it. And I'll file the papers this week."

"Good. And put this one on the fast track. He wants that money soon."

"I'll take care of it."

"I'm sure you will." Kyle headed toward the bedroom door then halted abruptly. "Hey, how's that new law firm working out?" he asked with a menacing smile.

"Fine."

"They keeping their noses out of your business?"

"Don't worry about it."

"Oh, I'm not at all worried about it. But *he* thinks you were a fool to make that move."

Tom's stomach clenched. "I had my reasons." Indeed, he did. Joining the firm was supposed to mark his final break from his dealings with all of this. The new firm was supposed to be a fresh start, where he could transition his clients to his partners before drifting off into an uneventful retirement. "And I was supposed to be done anyway."

"Done, huh?" Kyle scoffed. "Did you ever really think that was an option?" He pointed a finger at Tom. "You're done when I say so. And in the meantime, just be sure that none of your new friends start sticking their noses in my business."

Tom forced himself not to flinch. "They won't."

"Good. 'Cause if they do, then they'll end up like your client over there"—he patted the protruding grip of his holstered gun—"except it won't be nearly as peaceful."

Chapter 2

Jack Collins stood in front of a wall of windows and stared out at the Long Island Sound. On that clear April morning, sunlight bounced off the tops of an endless stream of wavelets, making the entire expanse from Greenwich to New York glimmer like a giant gemstone. He had moved his law firm to these offices almost three years ago, lured by the prestigious address and seduced by the priceless views. Despite a significant discount from the generous landlord, the monthly rent was probably more than he should have been willing to pay.

Indeed, the firm's finances remained uncomfortably tight. Fortunately, the firm's tax work provided a steady stream of revenue. The regular flow of sophisticated estate planning helped, too, a constant drumbeat of wealthy clients needing wills and trusts. Jack enjoyed a growing reputation as one of the state's elite estate-planning attorneys. But like any young firm, Collins, Warren & Oswald—better known as CWO—had only a trickle of the most lucrative estate-settlement work. The firm was simply too young to have enough of their clients dying off and providing the steady work of administering estates and trusts. As a result, every Monday morning, when the lawyers met in this conference room to discuss the work that would fill the week ahead, Jack silently worried that there wouldn't be enough, that his law firm would eventually fail.

The door creaked open, drawing Jack's attention away from the beauty outside the window. As they seemed to always do, Clay Warren and Steve Oswald entered one right after the other. The increasingly fit thirty-eight-year-old Warren had the healthy glow of someone who'd probably already jogged a few miles that morning, while the increasingly chubby Oswald had probably been packing school lunches and

shuffling children out the door. Warren's fitted shirt and pants contrasted with Oswald's flowing, outdated clothing, accentuating the physical
difference between the two men and artificially widening what was just
a few years' gap in their ages. Yet despite their many differences, they
remained the most loyal of law partners and the very best of friends.

Claire Reed followed a step behind the dynamic duo of tax lawyers.
Her long hair was gathered in a single braid that graced her right shoulder, dangling nearly halfway down the front of her red satin blouse. Although she was technically still a legal secretary, she was nearing com-
pletion of her third year at Quinnipiac Law, an achievement Jack and
his partners had decided was sufficient to entitle her to a seat at the
Monday morning meetings.

"So, the spread looks a little different," Claire said as she reached
the table.

The usual plate of muffins was adorned with a single candle. A bottle of champagne stood next to the platter with five plastic cups lined
up neatly beside it.

Jack smiled. "You don't miss a trick, do you?"

"I try not to. Anniversary celebration?"

"Correct again. By the way, anyone know where the guest of honor
is?" Jack glanced at the door. "We can't really start without him."

The question was met with blank stares and shrugged shoulders.

"Probably stuck on Lake Avenue in the Bentley again," Clay finally
offered.

The others chuckled.

That was a good guess. One of the estate planning bar's most re-
spected lawyers, and a good twenty years older than any of the others
at CWO, their newest law partner seemed lost in an earlier era. He always wore a coat and tie, kept his office filled with old books and dusty
antiques, and burned far too much gasoline driving to and from his
backcountry Greenwich home in a stunning, but exceedingly unreli-

able, vintage Bentley. "Car trouble," he'd often explain when stumbling in late for a meeting, which happened more often than not.

Yet despite his commuting challenges, he'd been a great addition to the firm. A member of the Greenwich bar for over thirty years, he was politically and socially connected in a way the rest of them could only dream of. The Greenwich elite looked upon him as a lifelong friend.

Exactly one year ago, he had brought his career's worth of experience, connections, and gravitas to Jack's upstart law firm. By joining CWO, their new partner had gotten a succession plan for his impending retirement, ensuring him a healthy salary as he transitioned his clients to younger lawyers. In exchange, the law firm had gotten a needed infusion of maturity and gray hair, along with the new client base. Their partnership had been a win-win, a match made in heaven.

"He's walking in now," Steve reported. "Just texted me from the lobby."

"Great." Jack checked the time on his phone. "At this point, we should probably tackle business first," he added before sitting down at the table. "Then we'll uncork the champagne."

The others followed his lead, quickly taking their seats and leaving the one closest to the entrance vacant for the guest of honor. They had barely settled into place when the conference room door opened again.

"So sorry to hold you up," the grey-haired latecomer said as he walked into the room. Dressed in his usual blue blazer and crisp tan khakis, he held his well-worn briefcase in one hand and a shopping bag in the other. After setting the bag on the table, he removed four identically wrapped boxes. "Happy anniversary, everyone." He passed the boxes around the table. "They're all the same," he added.

Jack untied the ribbon on his and removed the lid. "Wow, this is awesome." The lights reflected off a crystal paperweight with the firm's logo reflecting back at him. "I love it."

"I'm glad. And happy anniversary, all."

Jack held the paperweight in the palm of his left hand and ran the fingers of his right across the etched lettering. The gift was thoughtful and generous, a tangible reminder of the prestige his newest partner had brought to CWO. Changing his plans, he set aside thoughts of business. After carefully putting the paperweight back in its box, he stood and uncorked the champagne before filling the five cups.

Jack raised his champagne. As the others did the same, he offered a toast. "To Tom Nelson," he said, tilting his glass toward the honoree. "With thanks for everything you have brought to our firm."

Chapter 3

Judge Jessica Baldwin straightened the piles of documents lined up on the polished mahogany table. In her two terms as probate judge of Connecticut's wealthiest district, she had overseen the settlement of some of the state's largest estates. Today, she was dealing with another of those crown jewels, a half billion dollars passing from a well-known hedge fund manager to his surviving descendants.

It was no accident that she had ended up in such an enviable position. Decades earlier, when Connecticut had a probate court in nearly every town, the judges were little more than municipal officials. Over time, repeated waves of consolidation had reduced the number of probate courts by more than eighty percent. Most of the probate districts that emerged from that legislative activity contained three or four towns and were circumscribed by logical geographic bounds. But Jessica's district made no such objective sense. Instead, District Four was a gerrymandered arc of land that started in Cos Cob and wound its way through the wealthy backcountry of Greenwich, picking up some of the most expensive real estate in North Stamford and New Canaan as it curved through some of Fairfield County's poshest neighborhoods. The sickle-shaped district was colloquially known as the golden crescent, and to even the most casual observer, it had clearly been designed to minimize the workload and maximize the prestige of the judge elected to preside over this court.

Jessica counted some of Connecticut's most powerful politicians among her closest friends. District Four had been a reward for her loyalty. That gift would not be the last. By this time next year, she fully expected to be sitting on the Superior Court, the next step in her ascent through the judiciary.

While she carefully cultivated her reputation as a competent and thorough judge, she also knew her detractors would never be satisfied. To them, District Four was the very symbol of moneyed nepotism, with the well-connected politician presiding over the state's finest probate district.

One of those detractors was sitting across from her.

"So, a two-million-dollar proposed fee," Jessica said as she lifted one of the documents off the table and stared at the attorney who had represented the estate. *Two million dollars.*

In a more typical American town, such a number would be an eye-popping legal fee. But Jessica was used to seeing such numbers, and many far larger, in her courtroom. The proposed fee reflected three years' work overseeing an exceedingly complicated estate with investments around the globe. The team of lawyers and paralegals had spent thousands of hours doing that work and had earned every penny of the two million dollars.

But Jessica wasn't going to make it so simple for this particular lawyer. He was a sexist member of the old guard, a central casting version of the Greenwich senior partner, his wrinkled face and quaff of white hair commanding a deference she was not prepared to give. A vocal supporter of her opponent in the last election, he was someone who had never shown sufficient respect to her court. She had every intention of approving his fee, but on her timeline and on *her terms.*

Jessica looked at the smartly dressed woman setting next to the lawyer, the decedent's eldest daughter. "Are you happy with everything your attorney and his firm did for you and your family?"

"Yes, Your Honor." She tucked a highlighted strand of blond behind her ear, revealing a little of the mousy brown beneath. "They told me they would take care of us, and they have."

"So you and your siblings have no issue with their *quite significant* fee?" She smiled warmly at the client then glared at the attorney. *The power is all mine.*

The lawyer wisely sat silently in his chair, avoiding her gaze as he fiddled with the cuffs of his pinstriped suit.

"No, Your Honor, I do not."

Jessica turned her attention to the second lawyer. He was everything the other clown was not, a sandy-haired youthful ally who had consistently shown her the loyalty and respect her station commanded. She'd appointed him as the guardian to represent the interests of the minor grandchildren and great-grandchildren who had interests in the estate and trusts. "Your report indicates your approval of the proposed fee. Do you still approve?"

"I do, Your Honor."

That answer and the few hours' work needed to draft the accompanying report would earn the guardian a ten-thousand-dollar fee, a very generous remuneration. Jessica would never question *that* fee because the guardian was a friend of the court. Friendship had its benefits. *For everyone.*

"Okay then," Jessica said, leaning back in her chair. She took another long look at the attorney across from her. *You get it now, right? You understand that this is my house?*

The lawyer straightened in his chair. His lips parted for a moment, a thought seemingly about to emerge before he clearly thought the better of it. His posture softened again as he offered a silent nod.

"Well, thank you all for coming in," she continued after a measured pause. "I'm going to review everything one more time and then issue my decree."

The lawyer sighed. He again shifted awkwardly in his chair, his long-awaited payday still in doubt. The guardian raised his hand to his face, covering his smile and barely suppressing a laugh.

As everyone stood, the judge extended a hand toward the decedent's daughter. "I'm sorry again for your loss. And please don't ever hesitate to get in touch if I can be of any further assistance to you or your family. This courtroom belongs to the good people of this district. I'm merely here to serve."

Chapter 4

Jack stepped through the back door and onto the well-worn kitchen floor. As he slipped off his shoes and set them aside, he was greeted by the sound of laughter. He headed in the direction of the giggles.

Amanda lay flat on her back on the living room carpet, her arms stretched above her and a squealing toddler cradled in her hands. They both turned toward Jack as he entered the room, flashing matching smiles at him. More giggles ensued.

"Hey, honey," Amanda said. Wearing a purple Holy Cross sweatshirt and a pair of yoga pants, she still gave off a collegiate vibe, neither her face nor her glowing blond hair having lost any of their youthful luster.

"Hi." He knelt to kiss her forehead then lifted his son out of her hands.

"How's my big boy?" he asked as he hoisted Nate up to his shoulder and nuzzled his neck.

Nate's hair tickled his face. The sweet smell of baby shampoo wafted off the boy's wispy blond strands. Jack planted a kiss on the top of his head then set him on the floor.

Amanda stood and gave her husband a peck on the lips before pressing her cheek against his.

He placed one hand on the side of her rounded belly and wrapped the other around her back. As he pulled her close, he felt her growing abdomen.

"How was your day?"

"Kinda ran out of energy around three. I'm ready for maternity leave."

"Well, that's still a long way off."

"I know. I swear I wasn't anywhere near this tired with Nate. I'm getting old."

"That makes two of us. You know, if you need to, you can always go on leave early. We've got the money to survive without your income for a while." He wasn't completely sure they did, but this wasn't the time to tell her that.

"No, I can stick it out a few more months. I've got some cases I still need to clean up before I hand them off."

"Your call. You have any thoughts about dinner?"

"I was going to make spaghetti."

"You sure you feel like cooking? I can whip something up."

"It's spaghetti, Jack. It's not exactly a ton of work."

"In that case, it sounds good to me. Let me get changed, and I'll come help you." He turned to head to the bedroom.

"Oh, one more thing," she said, stopping him. "We really need to sort out this house thing. Once the baby is ready to come out of our room, we'll have no place for Nate. There's no way we can keep them both in that tiny nursery."

"What's wrong with the couch?" he asked, looking over at the lumpy blue-and-white striped sofa he'd promised to replace years earlier.

"Will you be serious?"

"I am. I've had some great naps on that couch."

"I know. It has the saliva stains to prove it."

"Those are Nate's."

She glared at him.

"Fine." He nodded. "I'll get in touch with Maureen tomorrow and ask for updated listings. Maybe we can see some more places this weekend."

"That would be awesome."

"You know what? Change of plans. Let me take Nate for a walk, and I'll grab some takeout on the way back. That way, you can take a cat nap. How's that sound?"

"Sounds like a great idea."

"Pizza?"

"Sold."

"Half peppers?"

"Yeah, but see if they have any red ones. They've been skimping on those lately."

"Got it. Give me a minute to get changed."

He headed toward the back of the house, unbuttoning his shirt as he went. Numbers jumped through his head as he thought about the wisdom of their taking on a maternity leave and large mortgage payment at the same time. But Amanda was right. Their current two-bedroom rental had been perfectly cozy when they first moved in, the outdated kitchen and small living room no issue for a working couple. But Nate's baby gear now filled every available corner of the place. For a family of four, it would be simply too small. Jack had dragged his heels as long as he could.

The math would be tight, crushingly so. But he had to make it work. *Somehow.*

Chapter 5

Tom sat in his office, two laptops and a steaming cup of Assam tea on the desktop in front of him. The scent of forest moss wafted up from the amber liquid. His partners had all left for the evening, but he was glad to stay behind. The silence was welcome, and the privacy was essential.

A feeling of shame slithered through him as he slid one of the laptops closer. The road to this point had started out with a small, yet fatal, step. Some faked invoices had been charged to an estate, and fifty thousand dollars had been slipped into his pocket. It had been a desperate response to a desperate time in his life, a momentary lapse during an otherwise honorable career. And somehow, he had gotten caught.

The one time Tom had crossed the line, the one and only time, Kyle Stone had appeared in his doorway, offering him his life's greatest choice: accept the consequences of his own poor decisions or sell his soul to the devil. He chose the latter, paying the resulting debt with secret wire transfers hidden by accounting tricks. He had kept his public honor by trading it for private shame.

In the beginning, he had thought it would be just one time. He was a fool. Like a recurring nightmare, the demands kept coming, one estate and then another. Samuel Heller would bring the total to seven. As the plan went on, the moral hole became deeper and deeper. The amounts of money he stole grew larger. The complexities grew as well: falsified probate accountings, unauthorized wire transfers, thousands—and ultimately millions—ferreted away from the estates of the dead. And that long, twisted road had finally led him to the perfect mark, the biggest score.

Five million dollars. That would be a tough number to make disappear.

As his stomach churned, he took a sip of the tea. The warm liquid flowed down and soothed his aching gut. He tasted caramel and nuts, the two flavors battling for supremacy before a hint of orange appeared at the finish. As he took another drink, he thought of the small English teahouse where, in what seemed like a lifetime ago, he had discovered the joy of tea. If he could go back there and start again, he would. But life offered no such chance.

He set the mug down on the desk and settled into the task before him. The laptop provided by CWO was running the official software used to track the assets coming in and out of Samuel Heller's estate. His personal laptop contained a private file showing the true records of Heller's wealth. When all was said and done, the law firm's records would show nearly forty million dollars coming into the Heller estate and an equal amount being paid back out, forty million dollars' worth of collections and distributions, a properly balanced account.

In truth, Heller's actual net worth at death was over five million more than Tom would publicly report. A skillful investor, Heller had his fortune spread across a number of investments. As Tom marshalled those assets, a slice of the wealth would find its way into the hands of Kyle and his unnamed co-conspirators, trickled out over time to numbered accounts, shell corporations, and anonymous organizations scattered across the globe. The widow would still get more than she would ever need, even after the modern grave robbers took their five-million-dollar cut.

Though Tom had worked the con for several years, he still couldn't name the other players. Kyle was the point person, but he definitely wasn't acting alone. At least one other person was involved, an unnamed *he* that Kyle would invoke whenever he tried to assert maximal authority. In the recesses of his mind, Tom had thoughts about who *he* might be. He had a guess, a *wild* one in every sense of the word, but he never dared pursue the issue. He knew better than to ask.

All Tom needed to know was that they, whoever they collectively were, had the goods on him. They knew about the debts. They knew how he'd stolen to cover those debts. If he ever crossed them, they would destroy him. Kyle had made it crystal clear that they, particularly *he*, had the ability to do so and that neither Tom nor his daughter would ever be safe if Tom stepped out of line.

So now it was time, yet again, to do their bidding. On his personal laptop, Tom logged into the estate's hedge fund account on the Excelsior website. The Excelsior account was the perfect partner for Tom's accounting smoke and mirrors, and from there, he'd take the largest cut. The Greenwich-based hedge fund catered to an ultra-private crowd, providing both regulators and their investors the bare minimum of required financial reporting while being notoriously rigorous in safeguarding the identity of their customers and their holdings.

When Sam Heller had first fallen ill two years prior, he'd designated Tom as his financial representative with Excelsior. Thereafter, only Tom had seen the quarterly statements coming from the fund. With the exception of those working directly for Excelsior, only Tom knew the true value of Heller's holdings.

After Heller's death, Tom had instructed the fund to liquidate Heller's interest and transfer the proceeds to the estate bank account. The account balance on the screen confirmed that they had complied with his request, sending over ten million dollars to Heller's account. Shifting to the firm's laptop, Tom input the transaction as a deposit of a little over six million dollars. Ten million received, six million reported. With those keystrokes, almost four million dollars had simply disappeared.

Keeping two sets of books was one of the oldest financial cons in existence. The fraud would be easy to detect if anyone dug through all the records and carefully compared bank records with the estate's court filings. But nobody ever would. When Tom filed the estate's final account with the probate court, all would look to be in order, with forty million collected and properly paid out.

Neither Heller's wife nor his son understood the details of Heller's far-flung investments enough to notice that the Excelsior assets had been underreported. The taxing authorities didn't care where the money went as long as they got their fair share. The judge would rubber-stamp what looked like a perfectly routine account. And since nobody at Tom's new law firm had any idea of his mastery of financial software, they would never suspect that he was keeping two sets of books and spearheading this type of structural fraud. It was the perfect crime. Or as close to perfect as he could manage.

Could he get caught? Sure he could, if someone dug deep enough. But the risks were his own fault. He could have stopped gambling long before he had. He could have stopped borrowing. He could have gotten help, *legitimate* help, declared bankruptcy, or stopped trying to pretend like his personal wealth had not all but disappeared. But he hadn't done any of those things. *Foolish pride. Fear of public ridicule. Inability to give up the nice clothes and fancy cars.* All of those had left him with no other choice.

And yet, for all of his efforts at looting the Heller estate, Tom wouldn't receive a single cent of the ill-gotten gain. All the money would go to others, to Kyle and his unnamed cronies, the silent beneficiaries of Tom's duplicity. That was part of the deal. And on one level, he was fine with that arrangement. He didn't want any of the plunder.

He just wanted all of this to end.

Chapter 6

Jessica Baldwin sped down the Merritt Parkway, her car's headlights providing the only source of light on the darkened roadway. She cranked up the volume on the Springsteen classic reverberating through the car and belted out the lyrics. She pressed a bit too heavily on the accelerator as she entered a winding curve. The tail of the car slid, pressing her awkwardly into her seat as she borrowed a portion of the other lane to keep the vehicle on the roadway. She reached a straightaway and floored it once again.

Flashing blue lights appeared in her rearview mirror.

Shit.

She tapped the brakes and eased over to the right lane. After popping a breath mint into her mouth, she looked back up at the mirror. The lights settled in behind her car rather than flying by as she'd hoped they would. She turned off the radio, plucked her phone out of her purse, and dialed a phone number.

"What's going on?" a male voice asked, the sounds of some sporting event clearly audible on the speaker.

"I'm on the Merritt in Stamford," she said. "I've got flashing blue lights behind me."

"You speeding?" came the reply.

"No more than usual."

"Been drinking?"

"A bit more than usual."

"Where exactly are you?"

"Just past Den Road, exit 33. Heading south."

"All right." He sighed as the sounds behind him fell silent. "Pull over and comply. *Slowly*. I'll get someone out there."

She eased the car onto the shoulder and turned off the engine. A bright light approached her from behind. As it illuminated the interior of her car, a trooper appeared at her window. She lowered the glass.

"License and registration," he said mechanically.

"Oh, of course," she replied, acting surprised by the request. "They're in my purse on the seat next to me. May I open it?"

"Yes, ma'am." He shined his flashlight on the passenger seat.

She opened her purse and slowly removed her driver's license and state judicial identification. She handed both to him. "Did I do something wrong?"

"You were going about eighty and nearly missed the turn."

"I know. Did you see that deer almost jump in front of me?" she said, placing her hand on her chest. "Good thing I had room to swerve."

"I didn't see a deer."

"Lucky you missed it then."

He looked at her documents. "Is this your car, Judge?"

"Yes, Officer, it is. Well, technically my husband's, I guess."

"Can you step outside of the vehicle, ma'am?" The officer opened the door, his flashlight searing her eyes.

"Of course." She carefully stepped out of the car. Her legs wobbled beneath her as she stood on the roadway. *Shit.*

"Ma'am, if I could just ask you to walk around behind the car. I'd like to administer a field sobriety test. Do I have your consent?"

Her pulse raced. "Of course. I've got a bad ankle though, so I may be a little slow."

"That's no problem, ma'am."

The back of her mouth suddenly went dry as she carefully moved behind her car. She had trouble filling her lungs as her chest tightened. Then blissfully, she saw another set of blue lights. The approaching police car pulled behind the first, and seconds later, a trooper emerged into the path of its headlights.

"Please just stay here a second, ma'am," the officer said as he walked back toward the second car.

The two troopers spoke for what seemed like an eternity before the first returned. The second one, wearing a master sergeant insignia, stood right behind him.

The first handed back her license and judicial identification. "I think you may have damaged your car avoiding that deer. It's probably best to leave it off the roadway until you can get it to a mechanic."

Huh? That made no sense. Then she remembered her story. "Yes, yes. I do think that's a good idea."

"My master sergeant here would be glad to give you a ride home, if that's okay, ma'am. I'll move your vehicle off the road and wait for the tow truck. We'll make sure it gets returned to you safely."

"That would be wonderful. I appreciate your help."

The first trooper pulled her car onto the grass while the master sergeant walked her back to his car.

"Thank you for coming out here to help," she said.

"It's our pleasure, Judge Baldwin. I hope Trooper Henry treated you well. He didn't realize who you are."

"He was perfectly polite."

"That's good to hear." When they reached the officer's car, he opened the passenger door. "You can ride up front with me if you like, unless you prefer the back."

"Up front would be great," she said.

Chapter 7

Jack walked through the front doors of Maplewood Gardens and caught a faint whiff of antiseptic. Despite its elegant private rooms and ridiculously high fees, Maplewood still smelled like every other nursing home.

Sarah Heller had been a resident of Maplewood since a few days after her husband's death. Jack wasn't entirely clear why she had summoned him. Tom was acting as attorney for and executor of her husband's estate, and that made her a client of CWO, a valuable one at that. But beyond that, she had no reason to even know Jack existed. Thus, her agitated phone call to his office that morning had raised a fair amount of curiosity and concern, both for her and for the reputation of the firm. With Tom out of reach somewhere over the Atlantic, it was worth the drive to northern Greenwich to try to appease her, to nip in the proverbial bud whatever crisis was brewing.

Jack had just checked in with the reception desk when he heard his name called from across the room. He turned to see the facility's executive director, Robert Granville, heading his way.

Jack offered his hand. "Good morning, Bob."

"Here to see Mrs. Heller, I understand." Granville flashed a smile, his teeth too bright for a man of middle age, just as his tan was too glowing for someone who worked indoors all day. "I understand Tom is on his way to Europe?"

Jack eyed the executive director, wondering how he seemed to know more about Jack's business than even Jack did. "He is, so I thought I'd pinch-hit."

"I'll gladly show you to her room."

"Thanks. Do you know...?" Jack began to ask Granville if he knew what was bothering Sarah Heller then thought better of it.

"Do I know what?"

"Oh... I was just going to ask where her room is, but you already said you'd take me."

"Indeed. Shall we?" Granville stepped away from the front desk and started down a carpeted hallway to the right.

As Jack followed, Granville slipped into the role of high-priced cruise director, greeting every resident he passed by name and offering some seemingly heartfelt compliments. "That's a lovely color on you." "I see you had your hair done today." "Your grandsons have gotten so handsome."

The residents, nearly all of them female, beamed or blushed in response to Granville's kind words, all clearly quite taken with the director.

Jack, on the other hand, wasn't sure what to make of Granville, who had spent much of his career managing golf clubs and hotels. The local lawyers thought it odd that Maplewood had chosen someone with no background in health care to run the storied facility. Jack wondered if the hiring was merely a sign that the nursing home, purchased two years ago, just prior to Granville's arrival, by a hedge fund, was now a business like any other. Granville had seemingly been brought on solely to market the nursing home to the Greenwich elites while career staffers actually ran the place. He was a professional glad-hander, that was for certain. But based on dealings with the director, Jack was fairly confident that the man's first focus was the well-being of the residents in his charge.

"I hope Mrs. Watson has been happy here," Granville said, referring to one of Jack's other clients.

"As far as I know, everything is fine. Perhaps I'll check in with her on the way out."

"I'm sure she'd love that."

They continued down the hall, the greetings and compliments flowing like water off Granville's tongue.

"We're here," Granville said as they reached a room nearly at the end of the hall. He paused and extended his arm toward the doorway. "After you."

Jack entered the room to find an impeccably dressed Sarah Heller sitting beside a man he didn't recognize.

The younger man stood and extended a hand. "Mitch Heller." After a pause, he added, "I'm her son."

"A pleasure to meet you," Jack said, shaking the man's calloused hand.

"Mine as well."

Jack turned toward Mrs. Heller and shook her hand gingerly. "It's a pleasure to see you, Mrs. Heller."

"Thank you for coming to see us. There's something that has me quite upset."

Clearly, she wasn't one to mince words. Jack had seen her only once before, at her husband's funeral. But from her demeanor and diction, it was immediately obvious that she was far more focused than she had been on that prior occasion. She stared straight at him. Her words were crisp and clear. Jack knew that dementia patients could have good days and bad. This day was apparently one of her better ones.

The son stood and offered his chair. "Please sit down."

"No, I'm fine." Jack walked over to the windowsill and leaned against it. He looked back at the doorway and noticed Granville still standing there. "Thanks for the escort," Jack said. "Could we have some time alone?"

"Oh, of course," the director replied, taking an awkward step back. "I'll be around if you need me."

Chapter 8

Jessica Baldwin stood in front of a glass showcase at Betteridge Jewelers, scanning a row of sapphire-and-diamond bracelets, each one more impressive, and more expensive, than the one next to it. Technically, emerald was the stone she should be picking out for her twentieth-anniversary gift, as sapphires were traditionally considered the gift for the forty-fifth. But she far preferred sapphires. And she had no plans for spending another twenty years waiting for them.

She pointed toward the far end of the row. "That one."

"How about I show you this one first?" the salesman offered, reaching for a bracelet near the middle of the display.

"No, thank you," Jessica replied. "I'd really like to see the other one."

"Of course." The salesman smiled. He lifted the bracelet from the case and clasped it around her wrist. "It's a beautiful piece. You have excellent taste."

"Yes, I do" was all the reply she felt he deserved. She dangled her wrist in front of the light and rolled it from side to side. The square-cut sapphires radiated an intense blue glow, the effect accentuated by the crisp white light reflecting off the colorless diamonds.

"It's an estate piece," he offered. "Ironic, I know."

"How much?" she asked, though she didn't care.

"Forty-eight thousand."

She paused, just for effect.

"But I'm sure we could do forty-five for *you*," the salesman added.

"Sold. Wrap it up." She beamed, admiring the stones one last time before handing them over.

Jessica had come a long way from that small town in upstate New York. The road hadn't been easy. She'd clawed her way to the top of her high school class then continued her upward path through college and law school, cobbling together a portfolio of odd jobs, financial aid, and loans to cover the staggering cost.

After graduation, she'd spent a few years in a law firm, whittling down her debts as she served the Greenwich elite, advancing the needs of her clients while exploiting every opportunity to pursue her own agenda. She paid her dues, developed her political network, and counted the years until she could achieve the status and power she had always craved. Then, mercifully, she met the man who would forever alter the course of her life. Unfortunately, they were both already married.

She had come to view her own marriage as something of a consolation prize. Andrew Stern was a loving man who provided all the support and security Jessica could hope for. He'd financed her campaigns and made the introductions that helped her become a judge. He'd put a roof over her head in Greenwich that she never could have afforded on her own, a lovely four-bedroom house abutting the Mianus River. Their home was not quite a mansion but was plenty big for just the two of them. And blessedly, he worked long days and traveled frequently, providing Jessica with the time and space to lead a life her husband didn't share. He was a good man who to this day still loved her more than she had ever loved him.

"Should we deliver it to your husband's office?" the salesman asked.

"I guess that's the proper thing to do."

"Try to look surprised when he gives it to you," he replied with a wink.

Surprised, indeed. There would be little surprise this anniversary: dinner at the usual place in the city, a stroll a few blocks uptown back to the usual hotel, and a drink at the rooftop bar, followed by exchanging of gifts, then back to the room for some perfectly pleasant sex.

It would be nice. Quite nice. But nothing more.

"Did you need a gift for him?" the salesman asked.

"Yes, and you know him. He's impossible to buy for. The man has more watches, cufflinks, and fancy pens than he could ever use. Anything else will just get thrown into a drawer."

"I understand the issue, but I have ideas. Do you want to look at some suggestions? We just got in a rather unique piece—"

"Actually, I think I already have something for him. So let's not worry about that now."

"Of course." He smiled. "Is there anything else I can help you with, Judge Baldwin?"

She looked at her watch. She did have a full five minutes before she was due at lunch just a block down Greenwich Avenue. And her guests could wait for her a couple of minutes if need be. As the salesman had just skillfully noted, she was a judge. "Actually, do you have any sapphire earrings?"

Chapter 9

Jack leaned against the windowsill. "Mrs. Heller, I know you're concerned about something with respect to Mr. Heller's estate. I have to confess that my partner Tom has been handling this matter himself, and he's on his way to Europe as we speak. So, I'm not sure I can really help—"

"We know Tom is unavailable," Mitch Heller said, "and that probably makes this easier."

"Tom's the problem," Sarah added.

Jack's stomach clenched. "What do you mean?"

"He's a thief," she snapped.

Mitch put a hand on his mother's arm. "Well, let's not go that far."

"I know what I saw." Her chin quivered as she spoke. "And what I heard. That bunch of clowns thinks the foolish old wife doesn't know what's going on under her own roof." She shrugged off her son's hand. "I may be confused about a lot of things, but I sure remember that day."

"Mrs. Heller, what day are we talking about?" Jack asked.

"The day Sam died, of course," she said, as if there were no other.

"And what exactly do you think happened?"

"Not *think*. *Know*. They stole his watch, Mr. Collins. I can only imagine what else they are up to."

"*They?*"

"Tom and that soldier he was with."

"A soldier?" This was getting increasingly bizarre.

"Yes, a soldier, a man in uniform, was there with Tom. They didn't know I heard them talking, but I did. I heard what they said."

"Did you ever talk to Tom about this?"

"Of course I did. He blamed Michaela, my nurse. What nonsense!"

Jack led the widow through the story a second time. He asked a few questions, but her recollection of events remained unchanged through the retelling.

Jack looked at Mitch. "Do you know any more about this?"

"Not really. I just came down for a long weekend, and the watch was all she could talk about. But the details aren't quite clear, as you can see. She started getting more and more agitated, and then she demanded that I contact you."

"Okay. So let me talk to Tom and see if I can figure out what might have happened." Jack forced a smile, hoping his offer might be enough to appease them for now. "I'm sure we'll work it all out."

"I know what happened," Sarah snapped. "That was a family heirloom, you know. A *Lange*. Made in Germany before the war. Sam came to this country with the clothes on his back and that Lange on his wrist. I want my son to have it. Mr. Independent over there doesn't want the house or any money. He should at least have something to remember his father by."

Jack watched her carefully as she spoke with logic and precision. She had either temporarily shaken free of her dementia, or she was now fully immersed in an alternate, deluded reality. He had no idea which it was. He was banking on delusion.

"Thanks for looking into this," Mitch said, his hand once again placed atop his mother's arm.

"I'm glad to talk to Tom about this, but let me make something clear. He's my partner and technically, as executor of the estate, a client. I can try to help clear things up, but if you're not comfortable with something Tom has done, you should feel free to file a police report or raise this issue in court. I just can't be the one to do that for you."

"Oh, I already talked to the police," she said. "They were useless. Probably in on the whole thing."

Jack's mouth fell open.

Mitch's jaw dropped. "Huh? Mom, you didn't tell me that. When did you talk to the police?"

"Right after your father died and I saw that watch was gone. Some detective came to see me. He asked a lot of nonsense. Lots of questions, mostly about Michaela. *How long was she with us? Where did she go? Did she leave on good terms?*"

Jack's pulse quickened at the mention of a police investigation that should have put the matter to rest. He was now convinced that Sarah Heller had slipped away from reality. He wasn't stepping any further into this mess until he had a chance to talk with Tom. "Let me get back to the office and sort this all out. I'll get back to you just as soon as I can." He shook their hands and turned to leave.

"That's a very special watch," she called after him, "not something you can replace, and it's not something that Michaela would've had any interest in taking back to Slovakia with her."

Jack's heart pounded, his efforts to calm the widow having failed spectacularly. He reached the door and pulled it open.

Robert Granville nearly fell into the room. "I heard yelling. Is everything all right?"

"Fine," Jack said as he moved past Granville and entered the hall. "Everything is just fine."

Chapter 10

J ack walked into the bedroom, a towel wrapped around his waist. A few feet away, Amanda was rifling through the top drawer of their dresser, muttering an uncharacteristic string of curse words. She yanked her jewelry box out of the drawer and dumped its contents on the bedspread.

"Shit," she said, her voice a bit louder.

"What's going on?" he asked.

"I can't find my second earring."

He saw a small cluster of pearls dangling from one of her ears. The other was bare. "The pearls?"

"Yeah. Oh Jesus, where are they?"

"Can I help?"

"No, you can just leave me alone," she snapped. She stopped and looked up at him. "Sorry. That was awful. I'm freaking out."

"I understand." He dried himself as he walked over to his side of the dresser. He slipped on a pair of boxers from the top drawer. "When did you wear them last?" A miserable failure to leave her alone.

"I don't remember. Last week, maybe. Saturday night."

Saturday night they had eaten at a small French bistro a few blocks away then come straight back to the house. "Did you have them both when we got home?"

"Just stop! Yes, I had them both when I got home."

He pulled a T-shirt out of the second drawer and slipped it on before walking back to the bathroom. He knew better than to ask again if she needed help. In fact, he'd already asked one time more than he should have. Maybe twice. Amanda was perfectly capable of looking for an earring on her own.

As he hung his towel back on a bathroom hook, he heard the words he had been waiting for.

"Oh, thank God." She walked into the bathroom, matching pearls in both ears and a broad smile on her face. "I don't know what I would have done," she said, dabbing a tissue against her eyes. She sniffled as she struggled to regain her composure, the rogue earring clearly having sent her into a tailspin.

"I'm glad you found them," he said.

Her hand was shaking. "Me too. God, that really scared me."

"You know, if they were really lost, you could have replaced them." He regretted the words as soon as he said them then winced when he saw her jaw stiffen.

"Replaced them?" She groaned. "These were my grandmother's. She wore them at her wedding. She gave them to my mother, who gave them to me, and someday, I'll give them to our daughter, if we have one. There's no replacing all of that."

Jack's stomach clenched. He had a pair of his grandfather's cuff links, two rather nondescript circles of white gold. They were long out of fashion, and he had never worn them, instead relegating them to the back of a dresser drawer. But Amanda's family was different. They were big into traditions, ritualistically passing down everything from jewelry to recipes from one generation to the next. He had lost count of how many Thanksgiving mornings had been spent in a frenzied search for a whole vanilla bean. The whole bean, as he learned, must be carefully distinguished from the more easily sourced extract, as was mandated by grandma's faded handwriting on a yellowed recipe card. Though it added no additional flavor to Grandma's apple pie recipe, at least none Jack could discern, the card clearly called for a whole bean, which often required a panicked last-minute supermarket run. The same grandmother's earrings now dangled safely from Amanda's ears.

"You're right," he said. "I get it."

A wave of nausea overtook him. Samuel Heller had been worth millions of dollars. But his family didn't seem to care about that, not in the least. Sarah Heller cared about her husband's wristwatch, a relic valuable not because of what it could fetch at auction but because of how it connected his family's past to their future. That watch was their whole vanilla bean, their missing pearl earring.

"Are you okay?" Amanda asked.

"Yeah, I'm fine. I was just thinking about something I need to do."

Chapter 11

Governor Daniel Milbank sat back in the oversized brown leather chair embossed with his name and the seal of the state of Connecticut. He smiled as the man sitting across from him shifted awkwardly in his seat. "What's on your mind?" Milbank asked, even though he knew the answer.

The chief lobbyist for Connecticut's one thousand gasoline stations dabbed a napkin against his sweaty forehead, even though it was a chilly sixty-six degrees in Milbank's office. "I'd like to talk to you about this energy package."

Of course he did. The series of bills just passed by the Connecticut General Assembly was touted as putting the state on the cutting edge of environmental conservation. The new laws would bring the state more electric trains, a steadier supply of wind and solar power, and a dramatic reduction in automobile emissions coming from Connecticut's overcrowded highways. A major feature of the legislation was a requirement that all regional gasoline retailers also provide services for electric and hydrogen cars, a mandate that supporters indicated would finalize the state's migration away from gasoline-powered vehicles.

"It's an incredibly popular bill," Milbank said. "Sixty-four percent approval according to my polls." He didn't mention the money that Connecticut's alternative energy companies, and their hedge fund backers, had funneled into his campaigns.

The lobbyist wrung his hands, and his cheeks reddened. "Popular, maybe. Until you lose half your gas stations because they can't possibly comply."

The point was a good one. The requirement that every station supply alternative fuels favored large suppliers with massive service stations. Although the tree-loving environmentalists who had pushed the bill through the legislature were likely too dumb to realize it, big oil was one of the major beneficiaries of Milbank's signature legislation. And big oil had been very generous to the Milbank campaign.

"There's no shortage of gas stations," the governor replied coolly. "In fact, we probably have twice as many as we need."

The other man grimaced. "These are hard-working people, Governor. You've got an unusual number of small operators in this state. We're talking the owner-operator, not some faceless corporation."

"Compelling! I love it!" Milbank slapped his palm on the desk then listened as the sound reverberated through the room. "The little guy. Small business. Just trying to eke out a living selling gasoline and cigarettes, maybe an occasional bag of chips here and there, right? Good angle. How'd that work with the legislature?" He leaned forward and glared at his guest. *I don't owe you any favors. You've done nothing for me.*

"Governor, this bill is going to hurt our existing energy industries," the man persisted. "It's going to cost jobs. Is there something we can do to avoid that? Some way to convince you to veto this bill?"

Hmmm... Was this about to get interesting? "Such as?"

"I'm just asking if there's anything we could do to encourage you to veto the bill?"

"What do you have in mind?"

"I'm not sure."

Too much dancing. I'm done with this fool. "You know, I got a valuable thing here." Milbank said as he lifted a silver pen off his desk and waved it in the air. "This pen, it's really quite magic. Somewhere down the hall, there's a nice leather folder with that bill inside. I sign my name at the bottom, and the floor falls out of your world. All your scrappy small businessmen will find the American dream isn't so easy. Poof!" He slapped his hand on the desk again, the sound echoing even louder than before.

"I understand, Governor."

"Your union really came out for my opponent in the last election," Milbank said, struggling to remain civil. "Lots of noise. Lots of enthusiasm. So good to see that level of interest in politics." He could feel his pulse rising as he pictured the signs and banners he'd confronted at his local gas station last election, the ones calling him "two-faced" and "corrupt" and the ones with a big red X running through his picture. There would be no dealing with these people, no chance at redemption for this lot.

"Yes, it did," the lobbyist said, looking down at the top of the desk.

Milbank twirled the pen in his fingers. "But you know what? That guy you backed? That guy you said would be better for your scrappy little owner-operators? Where the hell is he now?"

The lobbyist's face paled, turning a little greenish. "You have a lot of supporters in our ranks, Governor. Even if we endorse a candidate, that doesn't mean—"

"Oh Jesus, just stop!" Milbank pointed the pen straight at him. "I'm signing the bill. I'm going to sign it with this pen, and I'm going to think of your shining face when I do it. Politics is a tough business. Kind of like running gas stations, I guess. And I'm afraid your business is about to get a whole lot tougher."

Chapter 12

As an uneventful Monday morning meeting came to a close, everyone but Jack stood from the table.

"Hey, Tom," Jack said, his gut churning, "would you mind staying behind for a second?"

Tom sat back down. "Sure thing."

The others quietly filed out of the conference room, glancing back with curiosity as they passed through the door.

"What's going on?" Tom asked.

Jack swallowed hard. "While you were on your way to London, I got a call from Sarah Heller. She asked for me to come see her at Maplewood."

Tom's eyes narrowed. "That's my client, you know," he said, his tone accusatory.

"I know, and I normally would have just let you handle it. But you were unreachable, and Claire said the widow was super upset, yelling about how we had mishandled the estate, saying we were all a bunch of crooks. So I thought I should go try to defuse the situation."

Tom let out an audible sigh. "Did it work?"

"I'm not sure. Maybe. Can you tell me a bit more about what's going on with this watch?" Jack kept his tone casual. "It went missing or something?"

Tom shook his head. "That damn watch. Again? Really?"

"What am I missing?"

"This woman just doesn't let up. Where do I even start? A week or so after the funeral, the widow suddenly raises all hell about some watch that her husband owned but didn't even wear. It had supposedly been boxed up in a drawer for god knows how long, but it never showed up in the estate. She told me about it, and I brought in the police. They concluded that the maid probably swiped it on her way out, and the insurance company paid the claim."

"Well, that seems like it should have been the end of it." Indeed, this would hardly be the first time an heirloom had disappeared from one of the firm's estates.

"You would think. But all that's not good enough for her. So then she heads to probate court to make a big fuss about it."

"What?"

"Yeah. She drags me in to court over it. Thankfully, Judge Baldwin shuts the whole thing down. At least the judge understands it's not the first time a nurse pocketed something on the way out the door."

Jack eyed his partner. The story seemed perfectly reasonable, yet so very different than the widow's version of events. "So it was the nurse? Is that what the police concluded?" Jack asked, giving himself one last opportunity to evaluate Tom's reactions.

"Yeah."

"Did they track her down?"

"She's gone. Back to Europe."

"The widow was pretty adamant that the nurse wouldn't do it."

"Right, I'm sure. Taking care of Heller was a sweet gig for the nurse. I'll bet she wasn't too happy when it ended."

Jack was convinced. Tom's story all made perfect sense. A foolish widow had led him into a conversation he never should have started.

"I gave her a nice severance, too," Tom said, his tone indignant. "I thought that was enough for her to go back to Slovakia and live well, but I guess she needed a few grand more."

"A few grand? Is that what the watch was worth?"

"I think the insurance company gave us six thousand." Tom scoffed. "Heller was worth forty-five million, and the family is fixated on a watch."

"Fixated is the right word. Obsessed even. The widow is really convinced you stole it."

"I know. She's told me. Again and again." He slid up the right cuff of his shirt to reveal a gleaming gold Omega. "Do I look like a guy who needs an old watch?" In an era where watches had become just another form of technology, Tom owned a couple of classic, seemingly valuable timepieces.

Jack laughed. "No, you don't. Not at all. I'm sorry for sticking my nose into one of your estates. I just didn't see much of a choice."

"No worries. I get it. But are we done with this?" Tom's tone suddenly bordered on angry. Red splotches had blossomed on his cheeks.

What's that about? "Yeah, I think we've wasted enough time on this, right?"

"Right," Tom snapped. "So let's be done with it."

"Yeah, for sure," Jack said. "Hey, just curious, but what kind of watch was it? I think the widow said it was a Rolex. Any idea what model?"

His cheeks grew more crimson. "Why does that matter?"

"I don't know. Just curious. I mean, I might ask the good folks at Betteridge to keep an eye out, just in case someone tries to pawn it."

"An Oyster," Tom said, his angry tone now replaced by a hint of quivering in his voice.

"Mm-hmm." Jack jotted a note on the pad in front of him. "Isn't that the one Lyndon Johnson wore?" he asked, recalling some random trivia from his college political science coursework.

"No," Tom said steadily. "Johnson wore a Day-Date not an Oyster."

Chapter 13

T om strolled beside his daughter. He walked as slowly as possible down the pathways that twined around the college's gray stone buildings, trying to extend her impromptu tour.

She had chosen Connecticut College because of its strong program in environmental studies and because she'd been awarded a twenty-five-thousand-dollar annual scholarship. Picking the less expensive school was a generous gesture indicating that she suspected his finances were tighter than he let on. More generous than he expected given that she and Tom had maintained a rather cool relationship in the several years since Tom's contentious divorce from her mother. Now that his daughter was a maturing adult, Tom held out hope that they could rebuild their strained connection.

There was, however, one major problem with her choice of college. Just ten minutes up the road was the place that had cost Tom the life he once knew—his financial security, his wife, and ultimately, his honor. His daughter had no clue of the full magnitude of the damage Mohegan Sun Casino had done to his life or that he was still effectively repaying the debts he had run up years earlier. But she certainly knew that he had spent far too much time there during her teenage years, often returning home tired, angry, and far later than he'd promised he would.

For him, tonight's visit had been about trying to put all of that behind them, about burying the past pains and beginning a new future together. He had hoped that her settling into college would represent a fresh start for their relationship. She was returning his calls and texts, and she had enthusiastically invited him to visit her on campus. But while they had enjoyed a perfectly enjoyable dinner, it had not gone nearly as well as he had hoped.

Rather than fully welcoming him into her college life, she appeared to be keeping him a bit at arm's length. She had whisked him off campus before he could even meet her roommates. Conversation at dinner had been halting, their exchanges too often yielding to awkward silences and abrupt changes of subject. In the past, he'd often been too busy or distracted to give her his full attention. Perhaps she had come to accept that as the norm. She was strong and independent. If she'd ever needed her father, maybe she no longer did.

When they arrived at the front door to her dorm, she looked up at him and said, "I guess this is the end of the tour. I hope you enjoyed it."

"More than you know. That was an unexpected treat."

"I'm glad." She gave him a polite hug. "It was good to see you. And thanks for dinner."

"My pleasure. I like that place," he said, referring to the nondescript Chinese storefront in New London where they had dined. "Your shrimp looked great. I'll have to try that next time."

"Yeah, it was really good." She eased away from him and swiped her phone at the door to unlock it.

"I'm glad." He could feel the conversation running out of gas. "We can do this again if you like," he pressed, his heartbeat quickening as he spoke. "Maybe later in the month? You pick the day."

"Sure, sounds good," she replied without looking up from her phone.

He waited, but that's all she said. Just three vague words. Nothing definitive. No clear date.

"You're heading home, right?" she finally added.

"Where else would I go?"

She answered with a cold stare.

He suddenly realized what she had really been asking. "I'm not. I haven't been to a casino in years." *True.* "I haven't even thought about it." *A blatant lie.*

"Good, because Mom says that place is trouble."

Oh no, not the lecture. He wasn't up for another retelling of the story of how Dad cratered and mom picked up the pieces. He thought they were moving beyond that. She didn't understand what the casino had represented: a place where he could leave everything else behind and maybe, just maybe, feel the exhilaration of victory. She didn't understand the allure.

"Your mom doesn't know everything," he said, forcing a smile. He felt his throat tighten. Things were starting to go downhill.

"You hurt her, Dad. You hurt us both."

He hung his head. "I know that. I'm sorry. So sorry." He couldn't think of anything else to say.

"It's okay, Dad," she said, moving through the doorway. "Thanks for dinner." She gave a small wave and shut the door behind her.

"I love you." He said it too late for her to hear.

He walked back to his car and sat behind the wheel, thinking about what could have been, what *should* have been. He finally turned the key, and the engine roared to life. The radio blared Mahler's ninth symphony. He dispatched it with a slap.

He pulled away from the curb and drove down the dark road toward the campus exit, his high beams cutting a path through the foreboding night. A red light stopped him when he reached the main roadway. A left turn would take him toward the highway back home.

He turned right.

Maybe just a few hands. A quick hit.

Chapter 14

Tom stepped away from the cashier at Mohegan Sun and rattled five chips in his hand, each worth a thousand dollars. The first five grand of the night had lasted a mere ten minutes. His plan was to reclaim his losses and then get the hell out of there.

He weaved his way through the bustling casino, snaking through a series of blackjack tables before one caught his eye. From a distance, he noted that the dealer was an attractive blonde. As he stepped closer, it became clear that the blond wasn't real, but the attractiveness was. She looked older than he had first pegged her, late thirties, maybe even early forties. But no caked makeup. No smudging mascara. Unlike many of the others standing robotically behind their tables, she looked like she hadn't spent the majority of her life in a casino. *She was the one.*

A pair of twenty-somethings were sitting at the right side of the table, a stack of twenty-five-dollar chips in front of each of them. No doubt they were at a bachelor party or, more likely, some hedge-fund male-bonding night. A little good time with their best buds, probably drinking too much and unlikely to still be holding any of their chips in an hour. He scoffed, even though he was in no position to lecture on the vices of drinking and gambling.

He sat at the far-left side of the table, nodded at the hedge funders, and tossed a single chip on the table.

"One thousand," the dealer called out in an unmistakable Rhode Island accent.

The number attracted the attention of a corpulent pit boss typing on a tablet behind her. He waddled over to investigate and smiled at Tom greedily. He tapped some more on the tablet, then waddled back to his spot. A thousand bucks didn't buy as much attention there as it once had. In the old days, they had treated him like a king when he tossed a grand on the table, the high-end booze and comped hotel rooms deluding him into thinking he was a big deal. That was his undoing. The more they gave him, the more he tossed back, eventually sending himself to the brink of ruin.

He would be smarter this time. He would play in anonymity, declining the benefits of a frequent-player card. He would drink nothing but water. He would decline comped hotel rooms. He would just systematically play the game, pocket a few grand, and get the hell out. That was the plan. He was convinced he could do it.

The lady from Rhode Island dealt the cards. One of the hedge funders let out a whoop as a jack and an ace appeared on the green felt in front of him.

"Blackjack," the dealer said before tossing some chips and a smile his way.

Good for them. Though they probably didn't need the money.

Tom's deal, a fourteen, wasn't quite so generous, especially with the dealer showing a seven. He had to assume her total was seventeen, meaning his fourteen wasn't going to get the job done. He scratched a finger on the felt of the tabletop as his heart rate ticked up. "Hit me."

The dealer tossed an eight next to his four. "Twenty-two," she said as if he couldn't count for himself. She gave him what looked to be an earnest pout before sliding his chip away from him.

He swallowed a mouthful of saliva. She wasn't as pretty as she had been a moment earlier.

The next deal started off far better. A ten and an eight in front of Tom with a six as the dealer's up card. He waved her off when she asked if he wanted to hit. When the hedge-fund boys were finished playing their hands, she flipped over her card to reveal a king.

"Sixteen," she reported before pulling a five from the shoe. "Twenty-one," she said, again offering a little pout before she cleared the cards and chips off the table.

One of the men groaned. "You've got to be kidding me."

Tom felt a familiar emptiness settling into his gut. "You going to let me win one?" he muttered.

"Place your bets, gentleman," the dealer said, ignoring Tom's question as she swept her hand across the table. She apparently wasn't much for conversation.

Tom shook the three chips remaining in his hand and listened as they clicked off each other. For centuries, casino players had gone bust by thinking there was a pattern to wins and losses and that there was such a thing as a hot streak or cold streak caused by anything other than the laws of random chance. Even though he knew such thoughts defied logic, his quickening pulse told him his luck was about to change. He placed all his chips on the felt.

She tossed two kings in front of him and an ace face up in front of herself.

"No way," he whispered.

"Insurance, gentleman?" she asked.

Buying insurance was a sucker play. It gave players a chance to get their money back if the dealer happened to have twenty-one, but the odds said she didn't. He made the mathematically correct choice, the one the oddsmakers said a player should make. He shook his head when she looked his way and waved his palm across the table so that the cameras in the ceiling could register his decision.

She flipped over her second card to reveal a queen.

"Twenty-one." She again cleared the table of cards and chips.

The hedge-fund boys had seen enough. They thanked her, then after nodding at Tom, they stood and walked away. His pockets empty, Tom soon followed them.

As he passed the cashier windows, he thought about making one last run. He could take a cash advance and at least try to settle the score. But instead, he powered on.

Don't be a fool. Tonight's not your night.

Chapter 15

A knock on the door roused Daniel Milbank from a daydream. He swung his feet off the desk and dropped them to the floor. He'd enjoyed all of two minutes of solitude since the door had closed shut behind his last visitor, even though his daily schedule had promised him fifteen.

"Come in," he called.

His scheduler, Terri Jackson, opened the door. Although less than ten years out of Wesleyan, Terri was already one of the key members of his inner circle. She was far and away the best scheduler he'd ever had. "I'm sorry to interrupt, Governor," she said. "But there's traffic southbound, and we've moved up the departure for the Lawn Club. Five minutes. Is that okay?"

He smiled at how she'd made it seem like a question. "Five minutes is fine," he said as he gently waved her away with a flick of his hand.

"Great. I'll come back..." She turned away from him. "I thought five minutes," she said to someone in the hallway. "Okay, I'll let him know." She turned back and stepped into the office. "Actually, Governor"—her voice cracked—"they're suggesting you leave now. Can I help you get anything ready?"

"Not really." Milbank forced a smile. He stood from his chair and pulled on his suit jacket. "Speech is in the briefcase, and that's all I need." He stepped out from behind his desk, picked up his briefcase, and handed it to her. He ran his hand down the length of his tie. "How do I look? Everything straight?"

A uniformed state trooper stepped into the office. "You look great, Governor."

"Well, that's good to know," Milbank said. "What's with all the traffic tonight?"

"Business is booming. Low taxes. Good leadership." The trooper laughed.

Even considering the source, the words filled Milbank with pride. He *had* been a damn good governor. The state was lucky to have him. And tonight, he'd be telling just that to a room packed full of donors. He was moving their state forward, achieving things no other governor had ever done. They'd be lucky to keep him for another term.

"You sure you don't want to give the speech for me tonight?" he asked the trooper. "You probably know it by heart."

"I bet I do, but I'll leave the speeches to you, sir," he said, his formal tone in Terri's presence not all that different from the one he adopted during drunken poker nights. "I'll just handle the driving tonight, sir. Nothing wrong with a little overtime."

Milbank nodded. "Nothing at all." Indeed, overtime had served this particular trooper well, time spent working on a series of special assignments and the governor's security detail nearly tripling his base pay. "Plus, Terri tells me there's fillet on the menu tonight. Time and a half is even better when they serve a fine cut of beef."

"Yes, sir." The trooper grinned.

Terri, a vegan, didn't take the bait.

"Let's get moving before Ms. Tofu here gets angry," Milbank said, but he still drew no reaction from Terri.

They made their way down the hallway toward the main staircase, Milbank and his scheduler walking side by side while the trooper trailed close behind. As they neared the staircase, the governor's chief of staff hustled toward them from the other direction.

"Sorry, Governor. I was in the legislative wing," Brian Lockwood said before sucking in a deep breath. "I didn't know about all the traffic. You need anything else before you go?"

"No worries. We're all set. And the traffic is apparently all my fault, by the way. Low unemployment. Busy highways. At least that's what Stone back there says," Milbank said, pointing over his shoulder toward the trooper.

"I like that spin," Lockwood said. "You mind if we use that line?"

"Feel free." Sergeant Kyle Stone grinned. "I'm here to serve."

Chapter 16

Jack sat at the conference room table and waited patiently, allowing his partners to process the information he had just dropped on them. As was his style, Steve Oswald paced back and forth in front of the conference room windows, each of his heavy breaths and indelicate footsteps audible. In marked contrast, Clay Warren simply shifted in his chair, running his hands through his wavy hair.

"So that's what Monday was all about?" Steve asked. "After the morning meeting. Your conversation with Tom?"

"Yeah," Jack said. "I didn't think it was anything. But then..." His gut clenched as he replayed the conversation in his mind. "But then he said something that made me wonder."

"What exactly was that?" Clay asked, a hint of anger in his tone.

"He lied. He told me the watch was a different brand than it was."

"So he got the watch brand wrong? That makes him a thief?"

"It's Tom," Steve interjected from across the room. "Him getting a watch model wrong is like you mixing up two Lady Gaga songs." Steve's hearty laugh sucked some of the tension out of the room.

"Point well made," Clay said, flashing his white smile for the first time since he'd entered the meeting.

Steve made his way back to the table and dropped into a chair. "So Tom swiped a watch? Is that all there is? Any reason to think there's more to the story?"

Jack shrugged. "Who knows? That could be the end of it or just the beginning."

"Then, what's next?" Steve asked.

"I have no idea. That's why the three of us are here."

"Any idea who else might be involved?"

"Not really," Jack replied.

"Are you worried about that?"

"Terrified."

"Well, that's reassuring," Clay snapped, jumping back into the conversation.

"It wasn't meant to be. It was meant to be honest." Jack took a cleansing breath. "Listen guys, this could be a false alarm. Maybe there's nothing here. But where's there's smoke, there's often fire. And there's at least a little smoke here. So we need to check it out and see where it leads us."

"This isn't your fault," Steve said.

It was a magnanimous gesture. On one level, the situation *was* Jack's fault. All his fault. He had been the architect of Tom's joining CWO. He had been the one most convinced that Tom's presence would bolster the firm's sagging finances. He had been the one who pushed back against Steve's mild concerns and Clay's more significant ones. The three of them were fellow survivors of the scandal at R&H that had brought that storied firm to its knees. Jack worried he had led them into a new peril that might similarly endanger their new firm. The thought made his stomach turn.

"So what's the plan?" Clay asked.

Jack sighed. "I guess I need to audit his books. See if anything else looks amiss."

Clay raised an eyebrow. "And how exactly are you going to do that? He doesn't use EstateSoft, remember?"

That was a good point. While they held Tom out as a partner of the firm, his actual legal status was a bit murkier. He'd joined CWO on the condition that he could maintain separate banking and trust accounts for his own clients, preventing a true consolidation of his practice into their firm. Similarly, he still handled much of his own billing and recordkeeping, utilizing software he brought with him from his prior firm rather than the EstateSoft system that CWO used. The arrangement wasn't ideal, but Jack thought it would allow Tom to spend more time transitioning his clients to younger lawyers and less time on learning a new accounting system and software. The plan may have backfired.

"Claire," Jack said.

She was the perfect solution. She was smart and loyal beyond reproach. And as Tom's backup secretary, she had trained on his software.

Steve squinted at Jack. "Don't drag her into this."

Jack held up his hand. "I won't drag her into anything. She'll just get me access to the documents. I'll do the rest."

"And you'll keep us in the loop?" Clay asked.

"Of course. So we're agreed?" Jack looked around the table.

"Yes," the others said in unison.

"Okay." Jack stood and began gathering his papers. "I'll see what I can find out."

Chapter 17

Kyle made his way down River Road, the windows of his cruiser open to let in the clear evening air. He gazed up at the large colonials lining both sides of the street, instinctively eying doors and driveways as he drove past. Minivans were everywhere, basketball hoops here and there. The neighborhood was idyllic suburbia at its finest.

Kyle's own upbringing was far from so idyllic. His early years had been spent with a stressed and exhausted mother who struggled to provide for him and his brother while their father served his country, usually in places unknown and often in harm's way. When his dad finally returned home, the happy reunion Kyle had naïvely hoped for didn't occur. They all soon realized that his father had carried home a lot more baggage than the small duffel he left with.

Soon, Kyle's mother, no longer able to deal with the anger and outbursts, left for greener pastures. Dad turned to drinking and pills to dull whatever memories still haunted him. Money got even tighter, and to make ends meet, good old Dad resorted to selling some of those drugs. When a state trooper pulled over a teenage Kyle for speeding, the roadside stop ended with a search of Kyle's car and the discovery of a stash of drugs that only Kyle knew belonged to his father. Dad, pathetic to the end, denied knowledge of anything, and Kyle took the fall.

At age eighteen, instead of getting the football scholarship he'd worked so hard for, Kyle was looking at jail time, and he couldn't afford a decent lawyer. The public defender proffered little defense, and Kyle readied himself for the worst: a stint in prison, a criminal record, and a major roadblock dropped across what had been a wide-open path toward his future.

But the dark clouds parted when a judge showed him the kindness and mercy that his own father never had. "I see something in you," he had told Kyle. "I see great potential."

Behind the scenes, the judge pulled some strings and deployed some leverage. The charges were reduced. Jail time was averted. Kyle retained his freedom and his future.

The judge's kindness didn't stop there. He helped Kyle get into college by guiding him through scholarship and loan applications and writing letters of reference. And filling the void left by Kyle's own parents, the judge routinely invited Kyle to join his family for holiday dinners. With the judge and his family, Kyle found a second home, a place more inviting and more stable than the one he'd been born into. In turn, Kyle had become the son the judge never had and the brother that the judge's only daughter always wanted.

Neither the passage of time nor the judge's death had weakened that bond between Kyle and his adopted sister. He still saw her at least once a week, and she still made her home feel like his.

Kyle pulled into the driveway of her yellow colonial on the banks of the Mianus River. She stood waiting on the porch, a beer in each hand.

Kyle got out of his car and walked up the front steps. "It must be five o'clock."

"Actually, it's seven minutes past," Jessica Baldwin replied. "You putting in for overtime?"

"Nah." He took one of the beers and leaned over to kiss her on the cheek. "I'll give the people of Connecticut a free seven minutes today."

She chuckled. "How generous of you."

He took a sip from the bottle. "So, what's for dinner?"

"Trout. Some gorgeous rainbow trout."

"Fresh from the Mianus?"

"No, from the store. And given how much it cost, that fish had better be damn good."

Chapter 18

Jack called Claire's name when he spotted her walking past his office door. The sound of her footsteps came to a quick halt. A moment later, she was back in his doorway.

"Need something?" she asked.

"Yes, please. Can you do me a favor and get me access to the full ledger on the Heller estate?"

She looked at him quizzically. "Heller?"

"Yeah, I just kind of want to eyeball it," he said, trying to sound nonchalant. He glanced down at some papers on his desk.

"Okay. Sure," she said, confusion evident in her tone. She left his office and turned in the direction of her own.

That didn't go as smoothly as I hoped. Jack had heard the tension in his own voice, and she probably had as well. Plus, she knew full well that Jack was never one to care about the details of probate accountings, especially one from an estate he wasn't even handling.

Even so, asking her had been his only choice. If he could have accessed the records himself, he would have. But Tom's accounting systems weren't connected to Jack's computer. Only the two secretaries who worked with him could see those files. And of those two, Claire was the only one Jack trusted with this task. And he trusted her completely.

She returned a few minutes later with a thick stack of paper in her hand. "I just emailed you the ledger, but here's a hard copy as well. I know you like to kill trees."

"I do. Nasty little buggers providing all that shade and oxygen. Totally overrated."

She smiled. "Do you need anything else?" She took a step back toward the door.

Jack thought about letting her walk away, leaving her wondering what he was up to. But curiosity led to questions and rumors, two things that Jack was desperate to avoid. "Actually, do you want to do some on-the-job training?"

Her eyes lit up. "Of course."

"Great." He motioned to the chair across from his desk. "Swing the door shut, if you don't mind, and come join me."

After she'd settled into the chair, he slid his laptop in front of her and spread the hard copy across his desk. "I'll work with the dead trees. You can go electronic."

"Sounds fair." She adjusted the laptop screen, tilting it slightly.

"As you know, I don't normally review my partners' work," Jack said. "But Heller's nurse apparently stole his wristwatch. I'm kind of curious about what happened with the insurance claim on that. So let's find out. Walk me through it."

She frowned. "Through what? Which part?"

"The whole accounting. Start at the top. Let me see what you've been getting for all that tuition."

Claire accepted the challenge and began leading Jack through the various schedules of data, starting with the assets that had been collected thus far and detailing the distributions made and expenses paid. She obviously understood everything in the documents she was reviewing. Jack was impressed with her law school preparation. Her trusts and estates professor must have been at the top of his game.

She paused and scrolled back and forth between two pages of the account. "Well, that's a bit odd."

He leaned over to squint at the screen. "What's odd?"

"The claim on the watch."

His pulse quickened. "What about it?"

"Well, I see a line item for sixty-three hundred dollars going out to Mrs. Heller. It's marked as an insurance payment for the stolen watch."

"Okay."

"But I can't find any payment from the insurance company coming in."

Jack asked her for page numbers then flipped through the paperwork she'd given him. He set the relevant schedules side by side on his desk. He couldn't find the line item for an insurance payment either. "Is it on a different schedule?" he wondered aloud.

Claire shook her head. "I don't see it anywhere."

Jack scanned through the pages again. "Search for the terms 'insurance' and 'claim,'" he suggested.

She typed quickly. "Nothing," she replied.

He slid his chair back from his desk and looked at Claire. "So let me get this straight. The maid steals a watch. Tom pays the family out but doesn't seem to have collected on an insurance claim. That doesn't make any sense. And that's not what Tom told me."

She stopped scrolling and jerked her head back. "Wow, that's one of the stupidest moves I've ever seen!"

"I'm not sure I'd go that far. Tom might have some explanation. Maybe he just hasn't added the entry in the account."

"I'm not talking about Tom. I'm talking about Michaela Petroff, the nurse. She got a two-hundred-thousand-dollar severance, and then she pocketed a watch on the way out the door? Talk about stupid moves."

Jack's jaw dropped. "Two hundred thousand dollars?"

Claire turned the screen to face him and tapped a fingernail on one of the entries: *Michaela Petroff - Severance: $200,000.00.*

His mouth went dry as he stared at the line item. "Okay... yeah, yeah, okay." He glanced up at Claire. "You know, it all makes sense if the watch came first," he said, hoping she would take the explanation at face value. "The aide thinks she's getting stiffed, so she pockets the watch on her way out the door and then goes back to Europe. It could be that simple. So let's just drop it."

"Are you expecting that to work?" Claire asked. Her tone was bolder than most legal assistants would dare take with the managing partner. But Claire was no ordinary legal assistant. She was a future partner of the firm, well aware of both the goodwill she'd built up in her years with Jack as well as the leverage that came from being the stepdaughter of the firm's most valuable client.

"Am I expecting what to work?" Jack asked, taking one last stab at playing dumb.

"That smoke you just blew at me. You don't play poker much, and it shows."

"No, seriously, I—." He gave up mid-sentence. He was doing a lousy job bluffing, miserably failing in his attempts to insulate Claire from whatever happened next. Her loyalty was unimpeachable. She deserved, and could handle, the truth. "Okay. Something weird is going on with Tom, and that watch thing may or may not be part of it. But we don't need to figure it out today. So let's just sit back and see what happens. Make sense?"

She nodded. "Did you call Joe?"

"Not yet. I may need to but not yet."

She stared at him.

"Fine. I'll call him." He sighed. "But for now, let's just put this on hold." He piled up the ledgers and handed them to her. "Shred all this paper. And not a word to Tom. I'll keep an eye on this. For now, just forget any of this ever happened. Okay?"

She slid his laptop in front of him. "And you'll keep me in the loop?"

"Yes."

"Okay, then," she said, scooping the papers off the desk. "It's a deal."

Chapter 19

Perspiration ran down Daniel Milbank's back. His shirt collar dug deeper into his neck with every pulsing heartbeat. He had an almost uncontrollable desire to lunge across the table at Frank Fontana and kill the messenger.

"What the hell do you mean we could be *down* two points?" Milbank snapped. "Down two points to a damn *housewife?*"

His opponent, Alicia Williams, had been a state senator and attorney general before she stepped down to spend more time with her children.

"Well, Governor, it's still early in the race," the pollster replied, nearly robotic in his tone. "We're still months out, and more than twenty percent of voters are undecided. We also think about another seven percent are still in play, even though they claim to be backing Mrs. Willams. You could still win by a very comfortable margin."

This guy was as accurate as a weatherman, telling Milbank it was likely to rain unless it ends up being the sunniest day ever.

"So where do I need help?" the governor asked.

"The cities," Fontana replied without hesitation. "New Haven is weak. Bridgeport is *really* weak. If you look at the data here..." He put a sheet of paper on the table and pointed to a column of figures highlighted in yellow.

Milbank did his best to ignore both the spreadsheet and Fontana's babbling. Instead, he turned his attention to Brian Lockwood. "Who do we have in Bridgeport?" he whispered to his chief of staff.

"Well, Sal, of course."

"Sal? That's your first idea? The mayor who barely won reelection last time out after winning his first term by ten points? You want me to try to ride *his* coattails?"

"How about Price, the social worker?" Lockwood offered. "Wherever he leads, that community will follow."

"Now, that's a better idea," Milbank said. "A lot better." The popular preacher had the power to propel thousands of votes into Milbank's column, voters the governor was unlikely to have any other way to reach. "What does he need from us?"

"He's really concerned about public health. A community health center? A hospital expansion?"

"Yeah, great idea." Milbank snarled as his lunch creeped back up his throat. "Let's just walk on over to the legislature and get some bills passed. We should be able to start construction by the end of the day."

"We don't need to get it done before the election. But maybe if we promise to put it in the budget..."

"How long have you been in this job?" Milbank snapped. "Nobody ever buys 'We'll put it in the budget.'" He took a deep breath and forced a smile. "Thank you both for your time," he said to Lockwood and the pollster before pointing toward the doorway. "I'll take it from here." He then swiveled away, offering them a view of the back of his chair. *Meeting adjourned.*

Once the duo had left, Milbank grabbed a cell phone from his lower right desk drawer. In a world where his every encounter with the outside world was documented for posterity, a simple burner phone had proved to be a key lifeline. Taking that lifeline into his hand, he dialed the only person he'd ever been able to really count on, especially at times like this. "It's me," he said. "The polls are getting tight. Go see our friend Price in Bridgeport, would you? I want him on board."

"Got it. Any suggestion how?" Kyle asked.

"Let's start tapping the fund. Fifty grand. Or make it a hundred. Max. Not a penny more."

"And use it how?"

"Whatever he wants, get it. Stock his food pantry. Buy coats for the homeless. Just shove the cash in his bony little hands for all I care. But I want a full-throated endorsement. No hedging and no half-assed shit. If he balks, then Plan B him."

"Yes, sir. I understand."

"I knew you would."

Milbank tossed the phone back into his desk drawer and breathed a sigh of relief.

Weak in the cities, eh? Well, just wait and see what happens in Bridgeport.

Chapter 20

Jack felt a sudden queasiness as he dialed the number. He had delayed making this call for over a day. Although he was always glad to catch up with his college roommate, this time would be no fun. He was fully aware of the point of no return he was about to cross, the peril in which he was about to place his new law firm.

The call connected.

"Hey, bud. Good to hear from you," Joe Andrews said, his unmistakable Boston accent stronger than ever now that he was the special agent in charge of the FBI's Boston office. "How's the fam?"

"Doing well. Not long until number two makes a grand entrance. And you?"

"Keeping one step ahead of the bad guys."

"So, listen. I need some advice," Jack said.

"Uh-oh. You get arrested again? They bust your heroin ring?"

"No, the FBI will never figure that one out."

"I'm sure they won't. Bunch of dummies, especially the Boston crew."

They both laughed.

"Okay, enough with the bad jokes," Joe said, his tone turning serious. "So what's really up?"

"I've got a problem with one of my law partners." Jack cleared his throat as the point of no return slipped away behind him. "Some weird stuff is going on with an estate. I'm not sure exactly what he's up to, and I'm kind of stuck on what to do next."

"What kind of weird stuff?"

"The weird stuff you love to get involved in. An old watch went missing from an estate, but I'm wondering if that's just the tip of the iceberg. My partner didn't make an insurance claim that he should have, which is odd. Also, there's a payout to the nurse that looks fishy. I'm not sure what it all means yet, but there's something going on. I'm guessing there's enough to call it wire fraud."

Joe groaned. "Man, you really don't need this."

"Not at all."

"Does he know you're on to him?"

"Sort of."

"Great lawyerly answer. Care to explain?"

"I talked to him, yeah. I'm not really sure what is going on, so the whole conversation was kinda vague. I was just fishing."

"You catch anything?"

"Not really. Only that he lied. He gave me a story that didn't add up. I guess maybe he did steal this watch, or at least he knows who did. And he also apparently paid the nurse two hundred thousand on her way out the door, which seems awfully rich... and convenient since I probably can't track her down. That money could have gone anywhere. So it's a mess. Any thoughts on how I try to sort it out?"

"A missing watch kinda sounds like a job for the local police, doesn't it? As much as it would suck, you might need to call them in."

Jack winced at the thought of the Greenwich police marching into his law firm, the press and the bar association probably not far behind. "I'll go that route if I have to, but I'm not there yet. I don't really have any proof, nothing hard at least. So I'd like to try to sort it out a bit before I call in the cops."

"I think you did just call the cops."

"You know what I mean."

"I do. What you really need is a warrant to get access to his bank records or to set up some surveillance. If you want to go that route, I can connect you with New Haven to get that in place. You're in their jurisdiction not mine. But you're right that you'd need to get them something more solid first. There's no real probable cause yet. Your hunch isn't good enough."

"So I have to just sit back and wait to see what happens?"

"Maybe not. This partner of yours, you give him a firm cell phone?"

"Yeah."

"Good. You can legally track his calls. You can read his work emails too. Have your IT folks get you access. That's much cleaner than a wiretap and just as effective."

"Right. Good idea."

"Start there. Let's see what happens." He laughed.

"What are you laughing about?"

"I'm sorry, Jack. It's not funny. But I mean, talk about luck, right? Here you go again. Stepping right back into a mess."

"I guess so. Any last words of advice?"

"Yeah. Try not to almost get yourself shot this time."

Chapter 21

Daniel Milbank stepped out of the car and onto the Bridgeport sidewalk. His staff had done a good job of leaking word about his impromptu visit. A sizable group of well-wishers had gathered to greet him, a few reporters and photographers among them. A cadre of state troopers gently eased the crowd back as Milbank walked toward the Barnum Community Center, its boarded-up windows and soot-covered brick facade the only external signs of the fire that had recently raged within.

Marcus Price, the community center's director, was waiting at the foot of its front steps. A former state senator and a licensed social worker, Price had committed his fifty-year career to revitalizing Bridgeport and increasing services to its citizens. He was one of most well-connected and influential figures in this major urban center. Wherever he led, the community would follow. His pending endorsement would shift tens of thousands of votes into Milbank's column.

The governor waved at the crowd then walked straight toward Price, who looked older and frailer than Milbank remembered. The events of the last days had likely added to the toll being taken by time itself. The governor shook the man's hand as photographers circled around to get the best shots.

"I'm sorry to see this, Marcus," he said, making sure he spoke loud enough for others to overhear. "It's a terrible thing. A terrible loss for this community."

"Thank you, Governor, for being here." The director looked away then down at his shoes.

"Be assured that we will help you rebuild," Milbank said, directing his words more toward the crowd than to his host. "That's my personal promise. You know my administration has done more for this community and the great city of Bridgeport than any prior administration. And we are going to do even more next term."

Price nodded meekly.

Yeah, he knows. Message received.

Price led the governor up the steps and into the brick building. The press and public were held back by a line of troopers, leaving the two men alone in the fire-ravaged structure. The damage inside was startling. Soot blackened the walls and ceilings. Puddles of water still blanketed the floors. Entire rooms were unusable. *They may have gone a bit overboard here. But it was the director's fault, not mine. Price was the one who had played with fire.*

"I've been good to the people of this community, Marcus," Milbank whispered, making sure his voice didn't carry beyond the room. "I don't feel like my loyalty has always been repaid."

"I understand."

"But let's look forward, shall we? Let's think about the future. I think we need another firehouse on this side of town. I'm ready to fight for that. And a health center. And we will rebuild this community center, perhaps even better than it was."

Price nodded. "Thank you, sir."

"But I need your help. If you want these things, you need to fight for them, to fight for *me*. Do you understand?"

"Yes, Governor."

"Can I count on you?"

"You can." Price straightened his posture a little.

"One hundred percent?"

"Yes, sir."

"This is the time for your friendship, your loyalty. Are you with me in this fight?"

"Yes, *sir*." Price's tone finally hit the right note, the sound of complete surrender.

"Good, because we can do some great things together." Daniel leaned in close to Price. "And I don't want to have to come down here to tour any more burned-out buildings. You get it?"

"Yes, sir, I do."

Milbank turned and headed back toward the entrance, his pace deliberate. As he stepped back into the daylight, he put on a somber face. "This is a terrible thing that has happened to this community. I've come here to show my support, to show the good people of Bridgeport that I'm on your side. My administration is with you. We will fight for you." He raised a fist in the air as cheers reverberated through the crowd. "We will fight for more firehouses, for greater community services, including local, affordable health care. And we will help rebuild this crucial community center!"

He pulled Price closer and forced the other man's hand into the air. A sea of phones rose from the crowd, capturing the image that would soon permeate social media.

The governor shook Price's hand a final time before walking back through the crowd, the uniformed troopers helping to clear a path. He waved and hugged. He shook hands and posed for photos. He could feel the energy radiating from the crowd as he basked in their support. The people of Bridgeport were with him far more than the pollsters could ever see.

After his slow, triumphant passage, he turned to give one more wave to the crowd. The rear door of his car was held open by the senior trooper on duty that morning, the brass buttons on his uniform gleaming in the morning light.

"Nice work," the governor whispered to Kyle. "Price sure got the message."

Chapter 22

Jack and Amanda's real estate agent had been talking about the house on Highgate Road all morning. And for good reason. The Riverside colonial featured five bedrooms, six baths, and a view of the ocean from the living room window.

"Now this one is truly special," she said for the third time as they stepped into the house.

Standing in the massive foyer, Jack understood what all the fuss had been about. The house was finished to perfection. Its polished hardwood floors glistened in the morning sunlight provided by skylights two stories above. Ornate crown moldings and baseboards framed the room in lines of pure white. A dramatic staircase wrapped around an even more impressive crystal chandelier.

"You have to see the kitchen." The agent nudged them into the adjacent room. "That's a six-burner Viking," she said, standing oppressively close to Jack as she methodically detailed all the virtues of cooking with such a powerful gas stove.

"Do you mind if Amanda and I just stroll around a bit?"

"Of course. I'll be right here."

Jack and Amanda stepped quickly away from the agent and then slowed as they weaved their way through the first floor. Every room was painted in a different shade of white. Light streamed through large windows, revealing just a hint of blue in the living room and gray in the kitchen. The current owners had missed no details and spared no expense when remodeling this classic, a loving restoration done just right. Everything was new. Everything was perfect. Everything gleamed.

The price reflected all of that.

Buying this house would mean taking on massive debt. The mortgage would stretch their budget to the max. But the place sure would make a statement.

They went upstairs and were greeted by an equally impressive display. A long hallway led to a series of bedrooms, each one a light-filled oasis connected to an opulent bath. Once at the end of the hall, they entered the master bedroom. It was decorated in a palette of calming blues and connected to a marble-clad bathroom featuring a double sink, a steam shower, and a soaking tub looking out toward the ocean.

They moved back through the master and into the adjacent bedroom the listing called a nursery. The walls offered a hint of sky blue. A sea of greenery was visible outside the large windows. What a great start in life this sanctuary would offer.

Amanda made her way to the window, taking a long look outside before turning back toward Jack. "I guess we've seen it all. Let's head out."

"So, what do you think?" Jack asked as they walked back toward the doorway.

"We can't afford it," Amanda replied.

As they stepped into the hallway, the agent was waiting. The woman looked at Jack and pouted.

"Maybe we can swing it," Jack offered, generating hopeful smiles from both Amanda and the agent. "It's a stretch for sure, but we might be able to pull it off if we really want it." He wondered if he could convince a mortgage banker to agree with that assessment.

"Do we want to stretch so much?" Amanda asked.

"That's a really good question. No doubt this place is impressive. And five bedrooms gives us enough space for an office and a guest room."

The agent nodded enthusiastically, clearly ready to move forward without further discussion.

"And six bathrooms... Wow! That's really important."

Jack's sarcasm was clearly lost on the Realtor, who apparently could do nothing other than nod and smile. Jack couldn't think of six people in his life who would ever need to use the bathroom at the same time, much less in the same home. But toilets did add resale value.

The agent broke out of her smiling trance. "The furniture is negotiable. It was all hand selected by Minor & Watson."

Jack stifled a laugh at her name-dropping of the well-known Greenwich designers. The Collins' current apartment was furnished with mismatched hand-me-downs: a dining table from Jack's parents' house, a few threadbare Bokhara rugs from Amanda's, and the sofa that Jack and his law school roommates had rescued from a New Haven sidewalk a decade earlier.

"Amanda, was that the firm you had design our current place?" he deadpanned.

"No," she said. "But the folks we used really weren't all that good. We could use an upgrade."

"Minor & Watson are the best," the agent said, somehow managing to smile, nod, and speak all at the same time. "I bring them in on all of my luxury projects."

Jack followed Amanda as she slipped away from the agent and walked back into the nursery.

He stepped up beside her. "We should probably think about it," he whispered. "Are you ready to go?"

"Ah, sure," she said, without moving from her spot by the window.

The agent came into the room. "I know the sellers have one very good bid, but they are still actively considering other bids. Should we put together an offer sheet?"

"Why don't we go home and think about it?" Jack suggested.

Amanda finally broke away from the window and turned toward the door. "Yeah, we'll think about it."

"Of course," the agent replied, "but I wouldn't take too long to make your decision. There's lots of money in this town. A place like this is not going to stick around very long."

Chapter 23

Jessica Baldwin glanced up when someone knocked on her office door. "Yes?"

The door opened, and her clerk said, "The governor is here to see you."

"What?" she replied, her heart suddenly racing.

"Governor Milbank. He's here."

"Okay, okay. Give me a minute, then show him in." Jessica stood and smoothed the wrinkles from her skirt. She slid a mint out of the top drawer of her desk, popped it into her mouth, then crunched it between her teeth. Her throat burned as she hurriedly forced the candy down.

A moment later, Daniel Milbank appeared in her doorway.

"Good afternoon, Governor," she said with a deferential tilt of her head. She reached out to shake his hand. "To what do we owe this pleasure?"

He took her hand, cradling it gently and throttling back the strength of his strong grip. "Judge, the pleasure is mine. I like to visit our probate courts from time to time. I was on the Merritt and figured I'd come see you."

"I'm honored," she said. "Can I offer you a seat?"

"Give us a minute, would you?" he said to the aide who had trailed him into the room.

The aide, a lanky kid who looked no older than twenty, scurried from the room, shutting the door behind him. The governor walked back to the door and flipped the lock.

"Have you gone crazy?" she asked. "Showing up *here*?"

He put his hands on her waist, pulled her closer, and kissed her on the lips. As he bent further to nuzzle her neck, his stubble scratched gently against her face. A hint of musky cologne wafted up from the collar of his pressed white shirt.

"A little crazy, I guess." He raised his head and looked into her eyes. "I've missed you."

She smiled. "I've missed you too."

"Plus, I have good news."

He wrapped his right arm around the small of her back, pulling her closer. Their lips met again as he pressed his body against hers. His left hand moved down her front, sliding across the fabric of her skirt until he reached the hem and slipped his hand beneath it. Jessica's knees felt weak. It had been years, many years, since her husband had attacked her with such passion. And even then, having an investment banker in a passionate frenzy was not nearly as exciting as working the governor into a similar state. Especially *this* governor, with his piercing blue eyes and massive shoulders, the high school athlete who'd never lost his boyish good looks.

She pulled her head back and sucked in a lungful of air. "What's the good news?"

He grinned and pushed her backward until she felt her legs bump against her desk.

"Come on," she protested.

"A quick one," he said, almost grunting.

She put her hands on his broad chest and gave him a gentle shove that didn't move him an inch. "No way. What's the news?" she asked, repeating the question he'd invited then ignored.

"Marcus Price just endorsed me. We're going to clean up in Bridgeport."

"Oh, that *is* good news." She grasped his shoulders and leaned forward for another deep kiss.

He lifted her onto the desk and nudged her knees apart so he could stand between them.

"Danny, come on. I already look as hot and bothered as I care to. Let's save this for later."

"Later when?" His hands moved up the outsides of her thighs.

"Tonight?"

"Afraid not. This was a drive-by. UConn dinner is tonight."

"Oh, a room full of students," she purred as she reached up and caressed his cheek. "Better not take one home."

"I love it when you get jealous." His fingers crept under the hem of her skirt. "Not sure you've got the moral high ground there, *Mrs.* Baldwin."

She reached forward and grabbed him between the legs. "It's *Judge* Baldwin." She ground her lips against his then released her grip on him. "Show a little respect to the court."

He took a half step back. "I'd like to appear before the court." He laughed, clearly impressed by his own joke.

She leaned forward and kissed him again before hopping off the desk and straightening her blouse. He brought out the absolute worst in her. Almost every lie or cheat in the last decade of her life could be traced back to Daniel Milbank's terrible influence: the money that flowed out of her courtroom, the smoke of misdirection she blew at her husband, the secret meetings, the stealth moments, the handouts and payoffs. He had drawn her into all of that, in the process making her feel more alive than anything else ever had.

When they met, he had been a state representative, a devilishly cute one. He had a perfectly staid little life, at least on the surface: married to his high school sweetheart, two adorable children—a boy who looked like Danny and a girl who looked just like mom. The moment Jessica first looked into those piercing blue eyes, she'd known that the real Danny Milbank was nothing like the poster boy he claimed to be. Instead, he was master of playing the game, of working the deals, and of climbing the rungs of power. He was nearly as good as she was. Together, they would be unstoppable.

The first night, they'd ended up in bed. Over breakfast the next morning, everything else began. Over the years, he had eventually become governor, she had doubled the size of her district, and they weren't anywhere near done. A superior court judgeship was in the works for her, and being a senator was on his radar. After that, she wasn't sure what would happen. His kids would be grown. His power base would be unbreakable. Maybe then they would finally make a life together.

Then again, maybe it would be just fine, perhaps even better, for things to stay the way they were. The romance might fade away. The business deal would remain.

After patting her hair, she kissed him again then pointed at the door. "Back to work."

He went over and unlocked the door. "Oh, there's a little more news."

"Yes?"

"You're through Judicial Selection. You're on the next list."

That news was hardly unexpected, but the words still made her knees wobbly.

"Wrap it up with Kyle," he added. "It's time for us all to move on."

Chapter 24

The ultrasound technician leaned forward and squinted at the monitor. "Hmm." Her carefree smile of a moment earlier had slipped away.

"Is everything okay?" Amanda asked, raising her head off the table.

The technician shifted the probe and repeatedly circled one spot on Amanda's belly. "We're almost done," she said with what looked to be a forced smile. "Don't worry."

Jack noticed she hadn't answered the question, but he decided not to push it. He leaned forward and took his wife's hand, giving it a squeeze.

A few minutes later, the tech placed the probe in its holder on the ultrasound cart. "Okay, I'm all set here." She stood. "Just give me a few minutes, and I'll have Dr. Cunningham come in and take a quick look." She left the room before Jack could say anything else.

"Lisa's coming in?" Amanda asked. "I don't think she did that with Nate."

"I can't remember. I don't think so" Jack replied with feigned uncertainty. His throat tightened. "I'm sure it's okay."

After a minute of tortured silence, Dr. Lisa Cunningham stepped into the room, her long white coat flowing behind her. She seemed casual and relaxed, moving with no apparent urgency. She greeted them both with hugs, and Jack could feel his pulse slow.

Dr. Cunningham sat down on the stool the tech had recently vacated, slid it close to the exam table, and picked up the ultrasound transducer. "So, I hear everything looks pretty good."

Pretty good? Jack's pulse shot back up.

The doctor made a few passes across Amanda's stomach before settling in on what appeared to be the same spot the technician had become so focused on. She peered at the monitor as she moved the probe slightly to the left then the right, tapping at the computer keyboard after every slight adjustment.

What the heck? Jack's palms were moist. His throat was dry.

After a few more keyboard strokes, the doctor put the probe down and helped Amanda into a sitting position.

"Things look pretty good. Fluid level is perfect. The baby is growing really well. A few measurements are slightly off. Generally, I wouldn't even mention it, but the baby also has a small bright spot in its heart, an echogenic cardiac focus. It's not an uncommon finding, and it's almost always harmless."

"*Almost* always?" Amanda asked. "Could it be something serious?"

Jack reached out and took Amanda's hand. She squeezed his fingers tightly.

"It can be a sign of a heart defect, but I don't see any obvious structural issues to suggest that. And there are some studies that say it could be a marker for chromosomal abnormalities. Certainly not diagnostic, but something that suggests a slightly elevated risk, especially given a few of the other measurements we took."

Amanda gasped and put her hand over her mouth.

Dr. Cunningham shook her head. "Please don't worry. Your other testing and the rest of the ultrasound are really somewhat reassuring," the doctor added quickly.

Somewhat. Jack had heard that word louder than the rest.

"So what's next?" Amanda asked, frowning. Her eyes looked puffy.

The doctor sighed. "We should probably do a fetal echocardiogram. That's just another fancy ultrasound. It's a close call, but I think I'd also suggest an amniocentesis. That's also a relatively safe procedure that will give us even more certainty. But it's not totally risk free."

"What are the risks?" Amanda asked, her grip on Jack's hand becoming viselike.

"It can cause a little pain and some minor bleeding. Infection, of course, is a risk with any procedure. The biggest is a very small chance of fetal loss. But again, it's a really low risk."

Jack's heart was racing. Dr. Cunningham was trying to be reassuring, but the worst-case scenario filled him with dread. He glanced at Amanda, taking in her pursed lips and tense face. He could feel the pulse in her wrist beating as rapidly as his.

He put on his bravest face. "What do you think?" he asked his wife.

"I think we have to do it, right?" As she spoke, she looked at the doctor not Jack.

"It's probably the right call," Dr. Cunningham said. "Why don't we set you up for a follow-up ultrasound and amnio within the next week? We can get them both done at the same time. There's no real prep, but you'll need to rest for a good day afterward."

Amanda looked up at Jack. He nodded.

"Let's do it," Amanda said.

"Super," Dr. Cunningham replied. "We'll get you scheduled on the way out. And if you have any questions or want to talk through things some more, you can always call me."

"Thanks."

"Of course," the doctor said. "Please don't worry. It's probably nothing, but let's just rule some things out."

Probably nothing, she'd said.

Chapter 25

Kyle pulled into Jessica's driveway and cut the engine. He left the car and walked down the crushed-stone pathway that ran alongside the house and ended at a small dock on the Mianus River. The current raced by, providing an excellent workout for a family of mallards fighting their way upstream. Kyle grabbed a handful of pebbles and tossed them, one by one, into the water. The resulting ripples lasted just a second before they were subsumed by the passing current.

He heard footsteps behind him and turned. Jessica was heading his way, a can of beer in each hand. She smiled as she stepped off the pathway and onto the dock then handed him one of the cans.

He kissed her cheek then cracked open his beer. "How are you?"

She opened her can and took a hearty sip. "It's a wonderful day on the Gold Coast. How about you?"

"Clearly not as chipper as you seem to be. But still standing."

"That's good news. You're staying for dinner, right?"

"That was my plan."

"Good. Dear hubby's here tonight. I sent him out to get steaks. You can help him grill while you talk about football."

"Yeah, that would be great."

As husbands went, Jessica's seemed to be pretty decent, probably far better than she deserved. Certainly, dinner with Andrew Stern wouldn't be the most fascinating way to spend an evening, but he actually made pretty good company for a finance type, especially when he was providing the meal.

"So," she said, "where do we stand on Heller?"

Kyle scanned the riverbank to be certain they were alone. "Everything is on track. It's basically all done." He took another long drink from his beer as he studied her. She was different tonight, almost giddy. *What was going on?*

"Good," she replied. "Because we need to shut it down."

"Well, that's your department," he said, glancing back at the river. "Just get all your paperwork wrapped up."

"That's not what I meant."

When she didn't continue, Kyle turned to face her.

"I mean the whole operation," she said. "It's time to stop."

"What are you talking about?"

"I'm going to the Superior Court," she said, a tear forming in the corner of her left eye and rolling down her cheek. "Assuming Danny wins reelection, of course." She shed another tear. "We just need to wait for the next legislative session."

"Wow, congratulations." He hugged her, genuinely happy for her. Then his thoughts turned to himself. "So, what does this mean for me?"

"Nothing, other than this whole thing is over. We've gotten all the money we need. We did what we wanted. No sense in getting greedy. I need some time to clear up all these files before I leave the court. You can go back to being a cop."

Go back to being a cop. He didn't like her dismissive tone. He also didn't like the fact that the others had once again decided his fate. Kyle's neck was always out front, but Jessica always called the shots. Again and again, she'd expected Kyle to risk everything *he* had to further *her* agenda. She even *demanded* it, always reminding him that he owed her as much, that it was the least he could do. But it was getting to be enough.

"Fine, I can shut it down," he snapped. "But first, we need to talk money." He hadn't planned on going there tonight, but the time was right.

Her eyebrows drew together. "Is there a problem?"

"Yeah, I'm the one who's doing all the work, and I'm not getting my fair share."

"Your *fair share?*" she repeated, her tone again far too dismissive for his taste.

"Yeah, I never expected an equal cut, but there are things I need."

"Don't be a fool, Kyle. You know what I've done for you through the years. You've gotten a ton out of this arrangement."

His jaw tightened, tugging on the whole left side of his face. "I've gotten a *ton* out of all this? Yeah, a nice promotion. A lot of easy overtime. But that doesn't cut it. I'm the one who made *everything* possible. Without me, you've got nothing. And what do I have to show for it? I wouldn't mind living like this." He pointed at the massive house Jessica shared with just her husband as he thought about the one-bedroom condo he called home.

"So marry wealthy," she said, smiling. "It's worked for me."

"I'm not kidding." He balled his right hand into a fist.

"Neither am I." She smirked, clearly amused with herself. "You need to play the long game here. This was never about getting rich. *Nobody* got rich off this, including me. Look down the road. Trust in the plan. It's all going to work out just fine." She put her arm around his shoulders.

He pulled away from her. "Don't treat me like an idiot."

"Nobody thinks you're an idiot, so just relax," she demanded, dismissiveness now becoming patronizing. "Now, let's go up to the house and wait for my darling husband to fire up that grill." She tugged gently at his shoulders.

"So that's it?" He eased farther away from her. The judge had once again ruled.

"Yeah, that's it," she said. "It's over. Mission accomplished. Come on up, and let's get ready for dinner."

"No, thanks." He turned away from her and faced the flowing river. He chugged his remaining beer then tossed the empty can, watching it carom off a rock and tumble into the river, where the current pulled it downstream. "I've lost my appetite."

Chapter 26

Daniel Milbank sat back in the brown leather chair embossed with his name and the Connecticut state seal. He wasn't sure who had begun the custom of the governor's desk chair being personalized in gold leaf, but he liked it. Nothing says "I am important and powerful" quite like being the only one in the room sitting in a chair inscribed with your name.

Robert Dayton sat across from Milbank in one of the comparatively nondescript guest chairs. As a deputy commissioner of the Department of Revenue Services, Dayton was the state's third-highest-ranking tax collector. Before obtaining his current post, he had held a series of rather unimpressive jobs in compliance and corporate accounting, a background that would have never attracted the governor's attention had Dayton not served as treasurer of Milbank's first campaign for the Connecticut General Assembly.

Milbank had larger plans for Dayton. In his next term, he would likely offer Dayton the top job at the Department of Revenue. But first, Dayton had to prove his worth. Milbank had to make clear his understanding of what it meant to serve this governor and, thereby, the people of Connecticut. So after the obligatory discussion of Dayton's spouse and children, the governor pivoted to his agenda.

"You know I never meddle in my departments," Milbank said, notwithstanding his longstanding practice of doing just that, "but I'm getting a lot of pushback on how we're handling this whole thing with David Roth."

Roth, a local real estate developer and generous supporter of the governor's, was being audited for filing his taxes as a nonresident of

Connecticut, even though his family's phone records and social media accounts showed that he spent nearly all of his time in the state.

Dayton's lips quivered. "I'm sorry, sir. Pushback from whom?"

"A lot of folks in the business community. They don't like what you're doing with social media and all of that. Feels too invasive. A bit of George Orwell, the way you've tracked this guy."

Dayton slipped a finger underneath his collar. "With all due respect, Governor, I think our methods are sound. It's not like we're trying to make a poster child out of him. We've been treating this like any other audit. We've been completely fair."

That was exactly the wrong response. One didn't treat a friend of this governor like any other person. One treated this governor's friends with respect and dignity, bending in their direction as a sign of well-earned courtesy, not pulling against them in some woke attempt to appear evenhanded. This governor's friends were always under increased scrutiny, and that was anything but *fair*. If Dayton didn't understand that, he could forget even being commissioner. In fact, it would be time for him to go.

"Listen, Mark, I'd really like to see this just go away," Milbank said, trying to give his appointee a gentle nudge back on track. "I want Connecticut to be a place people want to be and to do business. That's how we keep this state a great place to live and work. You understand that?"

"I sure do. We need to compete."

"Exactly!" Milbank slapped his hand on the desk. "That's what our friends in Florida understand, and that's why they were eating our lunch for years. We can't compete with them on weather, but we can get rid of some of this crap that makes us a bad place to do business. Are you with me on that?"

Dayton nodded. "I understand, Governor. I assure you we're not trying to give him a hard time. We just want to collect what's fair."

Milbank's blood boiled as he heard that word, *fair*. He leaned toward Dayton. "*Fair*, eh? I do want you to be *fair*. I'd never ask anything else of you. But if you want to be a commissioner one day, you need to look beyond the narrow reading of statutes and think of the business climate. We need to reward those who are creating jobs and moving this state forward. David Roth is one of those people."

"I understand, Governor. I really do," Dayton said, now sufficiently supplicant in tone.

"Great," Milbank responded. "You know, you've got a very bright future ahead of you. I sure hope you don't squander it."

Chapter 27

Tom stepped outside the small brick building that housed the law firm of Bailey & Maldonado. He scrolled through the messages on his phone as he walked across the parking lot, looking up periodically as he slipped past rows of parked cars. His stomach dropped when he spotted a state police cruiser parked next to his car. Kyle Stone leaned against the hood. Tom tucked the phone into his pocket and walked toward the cruiser.

"Fancy seeing you here," Kyle said once Tom reached him.

"Just finished up a real estate closing." Tom was quite certain that Kyle already knew that.

"Come sit in my car for a minute." Someone who didn't know Kyle as well as Tom did might have thought the officer was making a request rather than issuing an order.

Tom rounded the car and got in on the passenger side, while Kyle did the same on the driver's side.

"How was your closing?" Kyle asked.

"Fine." Tom tapped his pockets, searching for a piece of gum to offset the sour taste in his mouth.

"Good. Got to keep those clients happy, right?" Kyle chuckled.

Tom said nothing. The sooner they could get past the chitchat, the better.

"So, Heller," Kyle said. "You're all set with that one?"

"I think my part is done," Tom replied as his pulse quickened. "I just need to prepare the final account."

"You may need to check your math again," Kyle said sternly. "I heard you're off by an extra million."

Tom tasted bile as his breakfast rose into his throat. Kyle's eyes fixed on his for what seemed like an eternity. Tom felt his eyes blink repeatedly. Kyle's never did.

"Another million?" Tom asked. "That's not what we agreed—"

"We *agreed*?" Kyle slapped his palms on the steering wheel then let out a haughty, dismissive laugh. I didn't realize we had to agree to things." He snarled. "Oh yeah. That's 'cause we don't."

"Well, you said—"

"Don't tell me what I said." Any hint of pleasantry was gone from Kyle's voice. "Just listen to what I'm saying now. Follow the damn instructions. And here they are. Another million. Right away. And then wrap it all up nicely with a bow. You got it?"

"Come on, Kyle. The math all works now. Nobody's got any issues. I wouldn't get greedy here."

"I'm sorry. I didn't hear you. I thought you might be calling me *greedy*."

"No. Not at all." Tom swallowed hard. "It's just difficult to move too much money. That's how people get caught."

"Kind of like that other estate, eh? Valkenberg. You remember."

Tom grimaced. *Valkenberg.* Kyle spat that name out every time he sensed the slighted resistance on Tom's part, reminding him again and again of how all of this had begun. Kyle always dragged things back to the time Tom tried to settle a gambling debt by misdirecting assets from Arthur Valkenberg's estate, a crime that Kyle had somehow stumbled upon when nobody else seemed to notice. In the years since, the price of Kyle's silence had grown and grown. He'd just added another million to the tally.

"I'll rework the figures," Tom said, the sickly taste now nearly unbearable. "I'll make it work."

"I'm sure you will." Kyle smiled. "And here's a little twist. This million goes to a different account. He handed Tom a slip of paper. "The info's all there."

"Huh? Why do you—?"

Kyle slapped the wheel again, the sound echoing through the cruiser. "For God's sake, just do it. No more stupid questions. Okay? Enough."

Tom's lips parted before he caught himself. "Okay. Got it."

"Good. Be sure you get it right. You can't afford to make any more mistakes."

———◆———

LATER THAT AFTERNOON, behind his locked office door, Tom scrolled through the Heller accounts on his laptop. He found an entry for two point five million and reduced it to two point four. He trimmed another entry by a hundred thousand. Line by line, he went through the ledger. A nip here. A tuck there. Finally, he reached the line item for the Excelsior account and sliced a cool half million from that total.

When all was said and done, the reported assets of Samuel Heller's estate were now a million less than they had been just a half hour earlier. Once again, Kyle Stone and whoever he worked for had gotten everything they had demanded.

Chapter 28

Jack was the last lawyer left in the building as the sky outside his window began to darken. Amanda was home, waiting for him and the Chinese food he'd promised to bring for dinner. Working as quickly as he could, he slid his laptop closer and began scrolling through the computerized records of Samuel Heller's estate account.

"I can handle it from here," he said to Claire for what must have been the third time. He had only needed her to input her secretarial credentials to get him access to the files. She hadn't been invited to stay beyond that.

"I recall you promising to keep me in the loop," she said from behind his shoulder, once again showing off her infallible memory.

"Yeah," he said as he moved through the pages, "but I didn't mean you could literally look over my shoulder and—"

"Ooh, that's weird. Wait! Go back to the top of that page."

"What did you see?" he asked, abandoning his efforts to shuffle her out of his office, instead shifting his chair so she could view the screen more clearly.

She pointed at the monitor. "The Excelsior Fund. The amount changed."

He looked at the line: Excelsior Fund: $5,600,000. "Changed from when? What was it before?"

"From the last time we looked at this. It was six point one million. It's down by five hundred thousand."

"Are you sure you're remembering that right?"

She nodded. "Absolutely."

"Is there a way to see a prior version of this?"

"No. It's pretty basic software. When the system updates, it rewrites over the previous files."

Jack sighed. "No backup at all? No way to see the version from a few weeks ago?"

"Only if you had a hard copy."

"Which I don't. Does Tom keep those?"

"Never... Oh, hold on. Remember the last time we looked at this and you gave me the paper copy to shred?"

"Yeah."

"I didn't shred it. I kept it to look at that watch thing more closely, to see if I could figure it out. I put the papers in my filing cabinet."

"Do you still have it?"

"I bet I do." She hustled out of the office.

She came back a few moments later with a triumphant expression and a slightly disheveled pile of papers in her hands.

"Amazing. Let's have a look," he said.

Jack flipped through the pages of the account and soon reached the one he was looking for. Six point one million. His stomach dropped. Being right had never felt this bad.

He slid the page across the desk. Claire swallowed visibly.

"Is there a good reason why that might have happened?" she asked.

"Sure. A bunch. Maybe the first number was a mistake. Maybe he typed it in wrong."

"That would explain it."

"Or maybe a half million just went missing from this account."

"How do you know which it is?" she asked.

"You audit. You go back to the source," he said. "Can you call the Excelsior Fund in the morning and ask for a copy of the statements for the estate's account? Act casual. Tell them you can't seem to locate it in the file and just need one for your records. You're just a secretary looking for some paper to toss into your files."

"Sure, no problem."

"Then we'll know."

"Do we want to know?"

"Now that's a really good question."

Chapter 29

Jack didn't expect this visit to the District Four probate court to take more than ten minutes or so. The judge simply needed to approve his final account detailing the handling of a relatively small estate. While there had been some family squabbles early in the estate, things had gone smoothly thereafter, and the beneficiaries had raised no objections to the final account. Yet, unlike all the other judges in Fairfield County, Jessica Baldwin required a hearing in such cases rather than just approving the account electronically. She loved summoning everyone to her courthouse in person, even if there was no matter in dispute.

Some lawyers said this proclivity for live appearances in her courthouse was a power trip. Others said she was helping friendly lawyers pad their bills, the hourly rates clocking away while they sat around her conference table, sipping espressos. Whatever the reason, Jack had no choice but to make the drive to northern Greenwich.

After Jack entered the courthouse, the clerk led him into what he expected would be an empty courtroom. He stopped in his tracks when he saw Jessica Baldwin already seated at the table, a cup of coffee and an exotic pastry on the table in front of her.

"Please come in," she said, pointing to the chair across from her. "Attorney Chin is running a bit late. Can I have them bring you something? A coffee at least?"

"No, thank you, Your Honor," he said before taking a seat as she had instructed. "I just ate."

Jack heard the door shut behind him, and his pulse quickened when he saw that the clerk had left the room. A faint sensation of nausea made him regret having wolfed down a sandwich in the car. They were flirting uncomfortably close with the ethical rules that prohibited one lawyer in a case from meeting alone with the judge.

"Your accounting is fine," she said, hurtling over to the wrong side of the ethical line. "As soon as Donald gets here, we can dispose of things quickly."

Jack forced a smile, but said nothing, desperate to avoid compounding the ethical violations.

"Oh, *ex parte* communication, huh?" She had apparently noticed his furrowed brow. "Do you ride?" she asked, changing the subject. She broke a corner off the pastry and popped it in her mouth.

"Bicycles?"

"No, horses. Like the ones on your tie."

"Oh." He looked down at the gift a client had brought him back from the Kentucky Derby a few years earlier. "No, never. Well, actually, one time in a national park, but I think that was a mule."

She nodded and picked up her cup. After taking a sip, she went back to picking at her pastry.

Just as the silence grew awkward, she spoke again. "I love to ride." She leaned back in her chair with a smile. "I don't do it much anymore. But when I was younger, we had fifty acres and a retired thoroughbred mare. My grandfather was a trainer." She pointed at his chest. "He would have loved that tie."

"Your grandfather trained racehorses? That's not something you hear every day around here."

"It wasn't around here. It was in Easton."

"Connecticut?"

"Actually, New York. Not far from Saratoga."

"I don't know it."

"It's a pretty small town. Blink, and you'll miss it, but we did have a ski mountain and a buffalo farm nearby."

"Sounds like an odd combination."

"Not if you'd like a good bowl of chili after skiing." She laughed, clearly far more comfortable with this conversation than Jack was.

She fiddled with the papers in front of her before looking back at him. "How's business?" she asked. "It's a tough thing, running a small firm."

"It is tough, but we're doing just fine, Judge. Thanks for asking."

"I bet things are a lot better now that Tom Nelson is on board. He's one of the best lawyers I've seen in this courthouse."

"He is a very good lawyer and a great addition to the firm." Jack shifted in his seat, increasingly looking forward to Donald Chin's arrival.

"That's good to hear. He's a good friend of this court. Has been through his long and distinguished career. You know, I believe in taking care of my friends and he's been one of them."

Jack's nausea returned. *What exactly was she trying to say?*

She looked at him pointedly. "I'm all about friendship. I hope you feel that as well."

A cold sweat trickled down his spine. "I do, Your Honor."

A knock on the door was followed by the creak of hinges.

"I'm so sorry, Your Honor," Donald Chin said as he entered the courtroom.

Jack rose from his chair to greet the other attorney. "Hello, Donald."

Donald nodded at him. "Hi, Jack."

"We were just talking about horses," Judge Baldwin said without rising from her chair. She broke off a corner of the pastry and slipped it into her mouth.

"Do you ride?" Donald asked.

"Not really," she replied. "But I used to as a kid."

Chapter 30

Daniel Milbank loosened his tie and walked over to the walnut bookcases that lined one of his office walls. He opened a small cabinet to reveal a crystal decanter and glasses. "Can I pour you one?" he asked. "It's Macallan 18."

"I'm on duty, sir," Kyle replied.

The governor laughed as he filled two glasses. "So am I. Come join me, would you?"

He moved toward the sofa and chairs, knowing Kyle would follow. Milbank took a long whiff of the whiskey and then a short sip. His taste buds engaged as the flavor evolved from the initial wood and oak to the lingering berries and spice. As he caught a final hint of orange zest, Milbank set his glass on the table and looked directly at Kyle.

The face of the aptly named Sargent Stone was devoid of expression and impossible to read. But apparently, he'd been far more loquacious with Jessica Baldwin when she jumped the gun last week and babbled like a schoolgirl about a judicial appointment that was still highly confidential. Kyle had reportedly responded with some harsh words, followed by a week of sick leave, during which time he had failed to answer his phone. His sudden silence had spoken volumes. Milbank had gotten the message.

"I'm sorry." Milbank's face started getting warm as he struggled to maintain a cordial air. Supplicating was not his strength, and he had nothing to apologize for. But tonight was about appeasement, not maintaining his honor. If an empty apology would help defuse the situation, he was glad to toss one on the table. "I *am* sorry," he repeated, hoping the words sounded more heartfelt without the contraction. "I

wanted to talk this through with you myself before anything was finalized. Jess just got a bit carried away."

"I understand," Kyle said. The generic response seemed no more
genuine than Milbank's apology.

Milbank lifted his glass and took another, larger swallow. He
moved away from his prepared remarks, veering, at least for the moment, toward something resembling candor. "Listen, Kyle. I didn't
mean for it to play out this fast, but we have come to an end of the road.
I did promise Jess a judgeship. I do have eyes on the Senate and what
looks like a clear path there. I do think it's time to wrap up our little
venture. We've gotten what we needed."

Kyle's expression softened. "I get it."

"But that doesn't mean I'm cutting you loose. Far from it." He
flashed a smile as he headed back toward his talking points. "I owe you.
And I'll take care of you. You want master sergeant? It's done. You want
a new assignment? I'll make it happen. Or I'll find you some staff job,
working with Lockwood. Whatever you want, I'll take care of you."

"Thank you, sir," Kyle said flatly. His face remained expressionless,
and his tone still seemed anything but grateful.

Give me a break. Milbank's impatience roared back in response to
what he saw as clear ingratitude. Kyle had gotten more than his fair
share out of this arrangement. He never could have passed the state
background check without Milbank's intervention. He never could
have just waltzed into Troop J the way he did, feasting on years of unfet-
tered overtime and the bloated pension that would come with it. The
man had to know all that. And Jess owed Kyle nothing more either.
Without her and her father, Kyle never would have found his way out
of Easton, New York. He'd gotten his fair share, whether he knew it or
not, whether he appreciated it or not.

But Milbank didn't say any of those things. Instead, he suppressed
his frustration and dug deeper to find some false sympathy to carry
him through to the meeting's end. "So, let's shut things down with the

lawyer," Milbank said. "Let him finalize things before Jess leaves the probate court."

"If you say so, sir."

Milbank nudged Kyle's glass toward him, and the trooper finally took it in hand.

The governor smiled. "Any other loose ends?"

"I don't think so." Kyle took a healthy sip from his glass, then set it down.

"And this lawyer will go quietly?"

"He knows the rules. He knows what happens if he breaks them." Kyle smirked. He was back on task.

"And if he does?" Milbank asked. "What do we have on him? He has a daughter, right?"

"His daughter. That's the biggest lever."

"And that's a good one. Think we need to send a little warning?" Milbank got a fleeting vision of a burned-out community center, which led to an involuntary chuckle.

"I don't think so." Kyle said, lifting his glass. "Not yet."

"And the law firm?"

"As far as we know, Tom's a lone wolf. He's not really integrated into that firm. Can't imagine he's given any of them a clue."

Milbank wasn't as convinced. "Can we keep closer tabs on them?"

"You want me to call the tech guys?" Kyle asked, his tone far more animated than it had been earlier.

"Yeah, that would be a good idea."

"And if they find something?"

Milbank took a long sip before replying. "Then do whatever you need to do."

Chapter 31

Jack looked up from his desk to see Claire in his doorway, holding a document in her hand. From the trepidatious look on her face, he knew exactly what the paper was and what it said.

"Excelsior?" he asked.

"Yeah." She approached his desk and handed him the statement, which was folded so that the last page was on top.

He checked the last entry on the page, the final transfer into Samuel Heller's estate. *Ten million?*

He looked at the number again then said, "*Ten?*" The amount made no sense.

"Yeah, I confirmed it with the account officer. I don't get it."

Jack didn't get it either. Ten million was a new number, different and far higher, than either of the versions they had seen on Tom's accounting software. Jack quickly did the math in his head. Tom's account was now off by nearly ten times more than they had originally thought. This was no accident, no mere typo.

What the hell is going on? Jack sat back in his chair and ran his fingers through his hair. He sighed as he pondered his options. He didn't like any of them. They'd moved well past a missing watch to something that looked far more like systematic fraud. He had no choice but to pull on this thread dangling before them, even though he had no idea what that would unravel and where it would lead.

"Where'd Excelsior send the funds?" he asked.

"To the estate bank account." Her eyes dropped toward the floor.

"Oh God. Constitution Trust?"

She nodded. "Yeah."

Jack shook his head at the irony. Tom frequently used Constitution Trust to open estate banking accounts, a choice that meant the same bank was now involved in the two great scandals of Jack career. "At least we know their general counsel," Jack deadpanned.

"I have her on speed dial."

"Can you set up a meeting? Confidentially."

"Sure. Of course."

"I'm sure they will be thrilled to hear from me."

"Last time worked out so well, with all the good press and stuff," she said, smiling impishly.

Jack laughed. As it always did, Claire's well-timed humor had dissipated the tension in the room. "Yeah," he said, "plus the fifteen-million-dollar fine."

"Fifteen million was nothing for those guys. Petty cash. They got off easy."

"I'm sure they share your view."

"I'll call them in the morning and set something up." Claire said, her tone back to business.

"Great, thanks."

"No problem. And look on the bright side. It could be worse," she said. "Way worse."

"Oh yeah, how's that?" Jack said, willingly taking the bait.

"Well, nobody's trying to kill anyone this time," she said, her smile broadening.

Jack laughed. "Good point. But are you sure about that?"

Her face tensed. "Actually, no," she said, her tone suddenly serious. "Not at all."

Chapter 32

One of Kyle's instructors at the police academy had taught him a life lesson he would never forget. "When you're heading into danger," the teacher had said, "always keep an exit at your back."

Kyle had taken those words to heart, and in the many years since, he had generally done a pretty good job following his instructor's motto. However, he had developed a blind spot with respect to Daniel Milbank and Jessica Baldwin. He'd never really thought beyond the obvious plan of moving forward with the two of them, of staying with the Connecticut State Police until he earned a pension or Milbank found him a better gig. He had never planned on making a retreat away from those two, foolishly forgetting to keep an exit to his rear.

But that changed today. With a few hundred thousand dollars of the final million Tom had sent his way, Kyle had become the proud owner of a small hunting cabin in Granby, Colorado. He could drop off the grid, literally. The cabin, fueled by solar and wood, was a rather nondescript structure lost amid the vast woodlands of the Rockies. It would be a strange place for Kyle to choose to run, but that was exactly the point. He'd spent one summer cleaning toilets and wrangling horses at the nearby YMCA, which provided enough connection to the area for him to know how to find his way around, but that was so long ago that nobody would ever think he'd found his way back there. It would be the perfect retreat.

The purchase had been made under an identity Kyle had borrowed from a state police database—Robert Gray, a banker from New Canaan—and funds were wired from an account matching that name. Kyle had hired a caretaker to keep an eye on the place and paid the man his modest fee for six months in advance. A small bag sat packed and ready in the trunk of his car. All the preliminaries were in place for a quick escape.

Kyle didn't expect to pull the trigger anytime soon. He wasn't ready to ride off into the proverbial western sunset. But at least he had options. He had an exit behind him, a clear path to retreat.

If ever he needed to, he could put this chapter behind him and start a brand-new one. It would be a retreat, but not one made in defeat. To the contrary, if he ever left, he'd do so as a winner, taking his fair cut of the loot with him, whether Jessica liked it or not. Even if his dear old friend refused to acknowledge it, Kyle had always been the brains of this operation. He was the one who had made it all happen. And if push came to shove, he'd reap his rightful share of the rewards.

They wouldn't dare come looking for him. He knew far too much. They'd have no choice but to let him walk away.

Kyle pictured the blue skies of Colorado's western slope, the wide expanses of aspen and cottonwood trees shooting skyward against a backdrop of snow-covered peaks. There, he could control his destiny in a way he hadn't since high school. There, he could make a fresh start.

For the time being, Connecticut would remain his home. His intent was to stick with this plan and to finish this job. But when the time was right, he'd be gone.

Chapter 33

Nobody at CWO was particularly good with technology. Fortunately, the firm had retained Legal Services Solutions to handle the tech infrastructure, from printers to laptops to cell phones. Periodically, LSS sent one of their so-called tech wizards to keep everything running smoothly. Moving quickly from office to office in their green polo shirts and dangling identification badges, they updated and debugged at lightning speed then moved on to the next task.

Jack stood at the side of his desk while one of those tech wizards tapped away on Jack's laptop. The man was at least two decades older than the twenty-somethings Jack was used to seeing handling such functions. His close-cut hair also contrasted with some of the scruffier employees Jack had come to expect, as did his military, almost robotic precision.

"You been with the company long?" Jack asked.

"A year or so, sir." He didn't look up as he spoke.

"And where before that?"

"The pentagon. And then the Connecticut State Police."

Jack knew it. The guy was out of military central casting. The thought intrigued him. Someone with that background seemed a bit overqualified to run software updates at a bunch of small law firms. *There's got to be a story there.*

"I got shot," the man offered as if he'd read Jack's mind. "Injured in the line of duty. Full pension. So I picked up this tech stuff part time. A little extra spending money." He'd clearly had to explain himself before.

"Thank you for your service," Jack offered, thinking he'd probably touched a nerve.

"Thank you," the man replied with no evident emotion. "May I have your phone, please? Unlock it for me if you don't mind, sir. There's a security patch I need to install on the encryption software."

"Of course. Sure." Jack typed the passcode into his cell before handing it over.

"Thank you. And I'm done with your laptop if you'd like your desk back." The man stood and walked a few paces away.

Jack noticed a limp. "Feel free to take a seat." He pointed at one of his guest chairs.

The tech raised the phone. "This won't take but a minute."

"Thanks." Jack sat down in his chair and began to scroll through his email.

True to his word, the tech laid Jack's phone on the desktop in front of him after about forty-five seconds. "You should be all set Mr. Collins. You've now got the latest and greatest security. If there are any problems, please call us anytime." The tech placed a business card beside the cell.

Jack picked up the card. "Thank you. I will."

"Very good. If you don't mind, could you direct me to Mr. Nelson's office? He's next on my list."

"Of course. Make a right out my door, and he's three offices down."

"Thank you, sir. I'll go take care of him right now."

The tech limped into the hallway and disappeared.

Chapter 34

Jack helped Amanda from the car and gingerly walked her up the stone path to the kitchen door. The follow-up tests all had gone as expected. Now, the wait began. Dr. Cunningham had promised that the results would be available in two days, maybe three. She had also tried to be reassuring, saying she expected good news and urging them not to worry. But as was her style, her optimism had been tempered by honesty. There was a chance the news would be bad, even tragic.

As they stepped into the kitchen, Nate bounded over toward them, his nanny, Patricia, trailing a few steps behind. Jack stepped in front of his wife and let his legs absorb the full impact of the barreling toddler.

Nate let out a big squeal as he collided with his father. He wrapped his arms around Jack's legs and looked up adoringly at his mother. "Mama!"

Jack picked him up and kissed his belly with a series of audible smacks. "Mama needs to go to bed. She needs to take a nap." He kissed his son again, generating more giggles. He then turned his attention to the nanny, who was gathering her belongings from the kitchen counter. "Everything okay here?"

"Yes, yes. He was a very good boy today. We made a big tower out of blocks." Patricia raised her hand above her head as she drew out the word big, generating another squeal from Nate. "He could probably use a nap too. Do you want me to put him down before I leave?"

"No, I can handle it," Jack said.

"Okay. I just changed him, so he's all ready for his nap. I'll see you tomorrow then. Eight thirty?"

"Yes, great," Amanda said. "Thanks for pitching in today."

"My pleasure."

As Patricia stepped outside, Jack turned to lead his wife and son toward their respective bedrooms, son hoisted against his shoulder and wife carefully walking beside him. The first stop was the master. He helped ease Amanda into bed then slipped Nate onto the mattress beside her.

"You need anything?" he asked as she stroked their son's hair.

"Nothing," she replied. "Just a nap. And then some pizza?"

"Both can be arranged."

Jack helped Amanda settle under the covers then picked up Nate and left the room, closing the door behind them. As he walked down the hallway, he lifted the boy out in front of him, making airplane noises as they moved. They flew into the small nursery, where Jack guided Nate to a soft landing in his bed.

"Have a good nap, buddy," Jack said, then he kissed Nate's forehead.

Nate grabbed a stuffed sheep and pulled it close, babbling at the animal in a language Jack couldn't comprehend. Nate had brought Jack the greatest joys and greatest worries of his life. So far, his future sibling was hewing the same path.

Jack quietly stepped away from the crib. "Have a good nap," he repeated.

Jack quietly crossed the room and turned off the light. He stood in the dark and listened to Nate's babbling a while longer before stepping into the hall and closing the door behind him.

Two days, he thought as he walked toward the living room. *Maybe three.*

Chapter 35

J essica Baldwin sat in her office, a half-eaten sandwich on the desk in front of her. No fancy lunch date today, no stroll down Greenwich Avenue. Just a quiet hour to regroup and reflect.

She looked around at the space she had occupied for the past eight years, the walls lined with framed photos and certificates accumulated during her two terms as judge. Running unopposed for reelection, she would soon enter her third term, one which she had no intention of completing. She was not going to spend her whole career in this courthouse. She was not her father.

Her father. He had devoted his life to public service in the truest sense of the phrase, serving some twenty-five years as a trial-court judge, all of them spent in the very same courtroom. His hours were long, his job demanding, and his devotion to the people of the great state of New York often stronger than his calling to his own family. And yet, when illness struck and he could no longer serve, that loyalty was not rewarded.

Disability coverage provided a portion of his rather meager salary. His life insurance and pension benefits were pathetic in comparison to those he could have accrued had he stayed in the private sector. And when he resigned from the bench and then lost his life, his family bore the economic consequences of his choice to pursue public service. His widow was forced back into the workplace. Jessica, a mere twenty-three years old, saw her dreams of law school slipping away.

But no matter the hardships, Jessica wouldn't give up on her dream. She borrowed much of what she needed for tuition. Scholarships covered the rest. She waited tables and bartended to buy her books, wearing outfits that would make her mother ashamed in places that often left her vulnerable and afraid.

Vulnerable and afraid. Two things she vowed never to feel again. So her path ahead became clear: go to a large firm, make big money, and grow her nest egg. She would take care of herself.

She executed that plan to perfection. She rose to the top of her law school class. She landed a coveted job at Fawber & Rhoades. Great salary. Excellent benefits. She was the envy of her classmates, on her way to the big time.

But her life at the large firm lacked one thing her father's career had always provided. *Power.* When Judge Charles Baldwin had walked into a room anywhere within fifty miles of Easton, New York, somebody recognized him, called him judge, and genuflected before him. And while he was always cordial and gracious in response, he relished the power. She could see it in his proud eyes and his self-satisfied smile. Even though Jessica never wanted to make all the sacrifices that came with her father's career in public service, she desperately wanted that power, that prestige.

And so, as she always had, she found a way to get all she wanted. She married for stability, not love, thus locking in at least some modest financial security. She aggressively paid her debts, freeing herself from the student loans and money woes that had shackled her to the big law firm and emboldening herself to pursue different dreams. And then, when the opportunity to run for probate judge fell into her lap, she saw it not so much as a calling as an opportunity. A chance for power and notoriety. A pathway to the prestige she had always craved.

She jumped at the chance. But she went in with her eyes wide open, seeing a judgeship not as some calling to ministry but as a bargained-for exchange. She would serve the public, but the public would serve her as well. This would not be the one-sided bargain her father had made. This would be a fair trade.

The next generation could always improve upon the work of the prior. And this Judge Baldwin, the second one, would enjoy both power and financial comfort. Her father had never seen the opportunity to do both or had been too self-sacrificing to pursue both goals. She lacked that character flaw. Plus, she was in the right town. There was no shortage of money sloshing around her court and community. There was enough for her to take a fair share from Samuel Heller and the other elites. And she had. *Millions.*

Of course, the funds weren't for her, at least not directly, and at least not right now. Marriage to Andrew Stern had provided a life of baubles and luxuries. She didn't long for extra cash, but she dreamed far bigger than life with Andrew. The funds extracted from the millionaires of Greenwich were for that bolder future, the future she now dreamed of between bites of ham and cheese, the one that included her and Daniel Milbank and a seat in the United States Senate.

In a few short years, a retirement would leave one of Connecticut's US Senate seats vacant, and Danny was already positioned as the heir apparent. The nomination would be his for the taking. But like the seat he now held, it wouldn't come for free. Milbank needed staff and infrastructure, both of which had to be large enough and ready soon enough to provide him an insurmountable edge. He needed the public support of a few key players, all of whom had their demands, their conditions, their price. Those deals had all been negotiated, the arrangements all but inked years in advance.

A few months ago, Samuel Heller's timely death had provided what would prove to be the last chapter in this story, and the final piece of the puzzle dropped neatly into place. The millions that Tom had been directed to skim from that estate would be all they needed to fill Milbank's campaign war chest, topping it off with enough to make him Connecticut's next US senator.

The scrappy kid from the inner city was now poised to power his way into the nation's political elite. Once he was settled there, everything was possible, for him and for her. And for *them*. Indeed, she could finally emerge from the shadows and join him where she belonged. By his side. In the spotlight.

She took another bite of her sandwich, the lettuce crunching between her teeth. *Enough daydreaming.* She slid the food aside and turned to her computer. After calling up the latest files on the Heller estate, she calculated what was left to do. Tom needed to wrap things up, then she needed to bury the evidence where her successor would never find it.

Her time as probate judge was running out. She still had a lot to finish.

Chapter 36

Kyle stood in the office doorway of Lisa Huang, Connecticut's chief medical examiner. She rolled her eyes as she pointed at the headset pressed against her ear then waved him toward the chairs across from her desk. He took a seat and waited for her to finish her call.

A couple of minutes later, she took off the headset and set it on her desk. "Sorry about that." She shook her head. "Don't even ask."

He raised one eyebrow. "I won't."

"So, what brings you here?"

"The guy from Avon," he said, naming an affluent Hartford suburb.

"I assume you mean the one they brought in this morning?"

"Yeah, that's the one. You work him up yet?"

She scoffed. "He's been here all of an hour or so. He hasn't even been assigned yet. Must be kinda important for your boss to have already sent you over."

"Local businessman and a friend of the governor's. It's just a situation we'd rather see fly under the radar."

"Ah. Now I get it. Governor's Pal Found Dead. That's not a great headline in an election year."

"Elections matter to all of us, you know." He looked around the office, noticing that what was once a wall of mismatched bookcases had been replaced with all new shelving. "This place looks better every time I come over here. The state's treating you pretty well."

"It is. And I appreciate it. But there's no politics in this office, right? You know I'll always do my job by the book."

"Of course. We're not asking you to do anything different. I'm just hoping you'll help keep the publicity hounds at bay."

"Got it," she said. "That, I can do."

"Thanks. Keep me in the loop?"

"Of course. We'll fast track it for you. And since you're already here, maybe you can just tell me what you think I'm going to find?"

"My guys said the scene was pretty clean. Nothing missing, no signs of any violence. Looks like he popped some Xanax that was laced. Street purchase."

"So you're thinking fentanyl? Good guess. We're seeing that showing up everywhere lately. We'll run a tox screen and see what comes up."

"Okay. Great."

"I'll assign it to Erin. She's good, and she's efficient. No drama. And she *hates* press conferences."

"That's exactly what we're looking for."

"I'll call you when we know something. If your hunch is right, it should be soon."

"Thanks so much. Anything I can do for you?"

"Nope. We're all set over here. I'll call you when I have something to report."

AS KYLE DROVE AWAY from the medical examiner's office, he dialed Mike Daly. Daly had spent much of his younger years as a narcotics trafficker and money launderer. In his semi-retirement, he'd found a new profession as a paid informant, systematically offering up information on many of his counterparts and their financial backers. Occasionally, Kyle or some FBI agent made a major bust thanks to Daly's tips, a citation or promotion often following. Also sometimes, like this week, someone who had crossed Daly showed up dead, the fallout of which his friends in law enforcement would help manage as a gesture of good will. It was a productive arrangement for all involved.

"You're all set," Kyle reported.

"You take care of things?" Daly asked.

"That's what I said. Just talked to the ME. She didn't bat an eyelash. She'll find the fentanyl and write it off as an accidental OD, and you're home free. One less competitor to worry about."

"Thanks, brother. I owe you one."

"Funny you should say that. I might actually need to collect. You able to meet later?"

"For you? Any time."

"Maybe my place? Around nine?"

"I'll be there."

"Perfect. And you still have the pills, right?"

"Of course."

"Good. We might need some."

Chapter 37

Jack paced across his living room rug, his phone pressed against his ear. Amanda sat at the other end of the room, leaning forward in her chair. Both hoped that his call to Joe Andrews would provide some magic solution to the problem that had brought them so many sleepless nights.

"I've briefed the guys in New Haven on everything," Joe said. "I can't say they sounded super interested. But it's on their list. They'll look into it."

"What does that mean?"

"It means they'll have an agent call you while they slowly start pulling together all the records and maybe do some quiet poking around. But nothing is going to happen quickly. It takes time to work this kind of case."

"So this could go on for months?" Jack looked over at Amanda and shook his head.

"Easily. Years, frankly. Remember how long it took me to get to Parker? This stuff develops slowly. You don't want to just jump and arrest the guy. You want to see what else he might lead you to. So just keep doing your thing. Monitor his emails. Watch his comings and goings. If he leads us to something really big, then things can move faster. If not, we slowly follow the trail."

"Is there any way we can get them to move faster?" he asked.

"Unless you find something else, not really. Right now, it's a lawyer skimming funds from a dead rich guy. Exciting to you, perhaps, but frankly a dime a dozen for us. Nobody's putting drugs on the street. Nobody's in physical danger. I hate to say it, but a wire fraud case is just not a priority. You might have more luck with the state police on a state charge, but no guarantee."

Jack frowned. What a mess he'd created for everyone. He was the one who had brought Tom into the firm. This was now his problem to fix. "I can't just sit around and wait for him to slip up. There's money missing. If nothing else, I need to tell the client and go to the judge, lay it all out there and let the chips fall where they may."

"You can always go that route. Or you can just wait for New Haven to get around to this. You've reported it to the FBI, so I don't think you've got any obligation to go to the court right now. Why don't you just sit tight a bit and see where it goes?"

Sitting tight had never been Jack's strong suit. "No other ideas? Just sit around, monitor his e-mails, and wait? No way to get this going faster?"

"I guess you could always try to bump him," Joe offered.

"*Bump* him?"

"Yeah. We have informants do it all the time. You say something vague to him to let him know you're on to him. Not too many details. Just apply a little heat, and see where he goes from there. If he's like just about every other guy in his situation, he'll panic and run to the missing money or the other players in the scheme. Just follow the trail he leaves behind."

"Does that work?"

"Almost every time."

"*Almost?*"

"Sometimes they hop a plane out of the country."

Jack laughed. "Tom does love London."

"And of course, there's always the risk that...."

"The risk that *what*?"

Joe sighed. "You need to be realistic, bud. This guy might just be skimming some funds, or he may be part of some larger operation. You knock over that beehive, and there's no telling what could come flying at you."

Chapter 38

Governor Milbank had been a great host for the members of Professor Krauss's political science seminar, twelve Yale College seniors who had spent the afternoon touring the Capitol. Milbank had walked them through the executive offices. He'd posed for pictures with the group. He'd engaged with each of them in turn, asking where they were from and what they were studying, while making customized comments in response to each student's brief biography.

Of the dozen students visiting that day, one had caught his eye right from the start. Melissa, a tall brunette, wore a navy-blue suit over a white blouse, the tight silhouette of both doing little to hide her athletic body and ample chest. He glanced her way again as the students coalesced around their professor.

"Governor, I think we should make our way out," Professor Krauss said. "We've taken enough of your time, and it's nearly time for dinner."

"Nonsense," Milbank replied. "It's still early." He pressed a button on his desk. "Terri, can you come join us?"

A moment later, the governor's scheduler entered the room.

Milbank gestured at the group. "We've got another half hour or so with these fine young people. Anything more they can see?"

"There's a press briefing that's still going on," she reported. "And the forum on the energy bill might run another half hour."

"That's great. Why don't you stick around a bit and check those out?" Milbank suggested to the students. "We can split you up into two groups. How about this? Terri, would you take any budding environmentalists over to the environmental thing? And Professor Krauss, you know where the briefing room is, correct?"

Both nodded.

"Oh, I assume this is okay with you, Professor?" Milbank asked, flashing a smile. "Dinner can wait a few minutes?"

"Of course, Governor. It's very generous of you. Thank you."

"You're very welcome."

As the students divided themselves into groups, Milbank worked the room one last time, shaking hands and posing for a few final selfies. He spotted Melissa sidling toward her professor.

"Oh, hey," he called out. "Wasn't one of you thinking about medical school?"

Melissa raised her hand. "Yes, I am."

"Terri," he said as he moved beside the budding physician, "can we see if Commissioner Bradley can come over to say hello to Melissa here?"

"Of course, Governor," Terri replied. "I'll swing by her office after I walk this group over to the forum."

"That okay with you?" he asked Melissa.

"Commissioner Bradley? That would be great." She beamed.

Brilliant white teeth. A nearly perfect smile.

The other students filed out of the room, leaving the governor and Melissa behind. Terri, the last one out, closed the massive carved door behind her.

"You look like you're an athlete," Milbank said as he guided Melissa across the room, toward the seating area. "What's your sport?"

She blushed. "Tennis."

"Great sport. I love it. But it's terrible for the shoulders." He put a hand on her upper arm. "You need to protect that rotator cuff."

He watched her carefully as he slid his hand across her shoulder and halfway toward her neck. She looked down at the floor. Her muscles stiffened. *Go slow with this one.*

He withdrew his hand and pointed toward the sofa and chairs. "Should we have a seat while we wait?"

She chose the sofa, perching on the edge as if ready to run. He settled into one of the armchairs across from her. Her skirt had hiked up as she sat, offering him a momentary flash of upper thigh before she grabbed the hem and slid it back toward her knees.

Pretending not to notice, he continued playing the role of would-be mentor. "So, let's talk more about your plans for next year. You're going to love UConn Medical School. I'm sure you know I've been a huge supporter of theirs. I bet no governor has done more for them than I have."

"I'm really excited to start there. Nervous. But really excited."

He leaned forward. "You'll do fine, I'm sure. And the dean is a close personal friend. I'll call her before you start and tell her to take special care of you."

"That's very kind of you."

"And if anyone gives you any trouble over there, you just remind them that you're a friend of the governor."

She flashed a shy smile, her cheeks reddening slightly. "Thank you so much."

Chapter 39

As Jack walked toward the CWO kitchen to grab a cup of afternoon coffee, he found the hallway to be unusually quiet. As he strode past dark offices and empty desks, the only person he encountered was Tom sitting in front of his laptop. Jack got his coffee then made his way back to Tom's doorway.

"Hey, Tom," he called.

The senior lawyer snapped forward in his chair. "Sorry, you scared me." He hurriedly shut his laptop. "Come on in and have a seat." He pointed to a seat across from his desk. "What's going on?"

Jack stepped into the office but didn't sit. "Sorry, but it's the damn watch again." He forced a laugh.

Tom didn't even smile in return. "What about it?"

"Do you mind if I take a peek at the insurance claim?"

Tom folded his arms. "Why?"

Jack's pulse quickened as he thought of the possible replies. *Because I'm the managing partner. Because all our reputations are on the line. Because whatever stupid thing you did is going to come back to bite us all in the ass.* None of those made it past the fake smile glued to his lips. "I'd like to see how you reported it. Just so I can put this all to bed."

"I'll try to track down a copy for you."

"Don't you have the file here?" Jack waved a hand at the far wall, which was lined with bookshelves littered with folders. He knew Tom's penchant for keeping voluminous paper files in his office. "A copy is probably in there if you can't find it on your laptop."

"It's not in there," Tom barked. He glanced toward the door then lowered his eyes. "I didn't bother filing a claim."

"You didn't file an insurance claim? Why not?"

"Because it wasn't worth the hassle. I'm billing the estate on a fixed fee, so what's the point in burning a lot of time going back and forth with the insurance company. So I just wrote a check. I'll take it out of my fee at the end."

You mean our *fee.* Tom's arrangement with the firm entitled CMO to fifty percent of the revenue he brought in.

Jack narrowed his eyes. "So that's it?"

Tom nodded. "Yeah. That's it."

On one level, that answer made perfect sense. Dealing with insurance companies was a major hassle, one which likely was not worth the time, given the firm's fee structure. So Tom's argument might have been perfectly plausible if it weren't for the other thing.

Yeah, that one other thing. "Can you tell me about the Excelsior account?"

The blood drained from Tom's face. "What?"

"The Excelsior account." Jack leaned toward the desk as he abandoned his casual tone. "Our books show a lot less than we received."

"What the hell are you talking about?" Beads of sweat appeared on his forehead.

"Tom, please." Jack's adrenaline surged, and his body tensed. "I can access the accounting software. You show a receipt of a half million less than Excelsior actually sent us," Jack said, intentionally revealing only a sliver of what he knew.

"That can't be right," Tom scoffed. "I must have input that wrong. I haven't finalized anything."

Jack shook his head. He'd seen enough to know the numbers weren't due to some innocent typo. "You changed the entry. It was over six million. Then you took a half million off."

Tom's face was crimson. He jumped to his feet. "What exactly are you accusing me of?"

Jack refused to back down. "We can work all this out, but you have to come clean with me. I know this isn't just a record-keeping problem.

The watch. The money. You're just not that sloppy. So what's really going on?"

Tom sighed and fell back into his chair. "I didn't take a dime."

"Tom, really—"

"Seriously, Jack." Tom's lips started to quiver. "Sarah Heller has more money than she will ever use. Just let this be. Don't mess with this. Don't mess with these people."

Jack's stomach muscles tensed. *These people?* "Don't mess with who? What the hell is going on?"

Tom got up and began to pace in front of his window, retracing the same path like a lion trapped in an undersized cage. Jack had expected either a stonewall or a tearful confession. But this was something different. This was panic, agony.

"Tom, what are you involved with?"

Tom stopped and pointed at Jack. "You have to drop this." His tone was approaching frantic. "Please just walk away. I'll get that half million back. I promise. But just drop it."

"You know I can't do that."

"If you keep digging, you'll cost everyone everything." Tom seemed to be on the verge of tears. "You'll get Sarah Heller a little more money, but *you'll* lose everything in the process. Everything you've worked for will be gone."

Jack raised his eyebrows as a small surge of anger coursed through him. "Are you threatening me?"

"Not at all." A tear ran down Tom's left cheek. "I'm *warning* you. There's only one way out of this, and that's to let me do what I need to do."

"Tom, I—"

"Please, Jack. Please. Let's just drop this."

"No. I'm not doing that. I want an accounting. A full explanation. In writing. Take a couple days, but I want to know exactly what went on here, and then we'll decide what to do."

"You don't—"

"I do!" Jack slammed his hand down on Tom's desk then pointed at Tom. "Take a few days. Get a lawyer, if you think you need one. But I want a full accounting of everything."

"Okay, okay. I'm going to straighten it all out. Just give me a few days to fix this."

"Fine, but you're on leave until this gets cleared up. I'm having IT shut down your computer access."

"I'll straighten it out," Tom repeated. "I really will."

Chapter 40

Daniel Milbank tried to figure out why he was so captivated by the college girl sitting across from him. It was not simply her looks, although she was truly beautiful. Perhaps it was her age, which was less than half his own, a source of vitality waiting for him to tap. But most of all, he realized, it was her innocence, her youthful exuberance when she spoke of her plans for the rest of college and beyond, the way she looked at him with adoring eyes when he offered his assistance, completely naïve about the bargain he would expect her to make.

A knock sounded.

Several seconds later, Terri, the scheduler, opened the door. "I'm sorry, Governor. Commissioner Bradley is gone for the day."

"Well, that's too bad. Thanks for letting us know. We'll come up with another plan." He waved her away.

Terri left, closing the door behind her.

"Well, so much for that idea," Melissa said, starting to rise from the sofa while using one hand to hold down the hem of her skirt. "I should probably join up with my classmates."

Milbank jumped to his feet. "That sofa can get a little low," he said, grabbing her free hand to assist her. He tugged her across the room, enjoying the feel of her soft skin. "Come here for a second."

When they were at his desk, he let go of her hand and plucked a business card from a holder. Flipping it over, he scribbled a number on the back. "You call me anytime," he said as he handed her the card, turned so she could see his cell phone number written on the reverse. "You've made quite an impression on me today. I'd be glad to help you in any way I can."

There was another knock on the door. Milbank ignored it, his eyes fixed on Melissa.

"Thank you." She took a step toward the door. "I really should go."

"There's no limit to what I can do for you." Melissa was now looking right at him, her eyes wide with adoration. He felt it. The feelings were mutual. He moved toward her.

She slipped sideways toward the door. "I should be going," she said.

Though her tone didn't show it, Milbank knew she didn't really want to leave. He wrapped his right hand around her wrist, gently at first, then tightened his grip enough to restrict her movements. He pulled her toward him and kissed her cheek. She didn't move, so he pressed his lips to hers. They were soft and wet. So young. So nubile. He slid his left hand down the outside of her leg.

His head jerked back as she slammed her hands into his chest.

"Stop it! Keep your hands to yourself!"

He was stunned. *What the hell?* "I'm... I'm sorry," he stammered. "I was just being friendly."

"That's not friendly," she spat, her tone now anything but submissive. Any illusion of innocence had been fully dispelled. She flicked his business card to the floor as she stormed across the room. "Don't you *ever* do that again. To *anyone.*"

After another knock, the door opened just as Melissa reached it. Terri stood in the opening, her mouth agape.

Melissa marched past the scheduler. "Tell your boss to keep his hands to himself," she fumed as she stormed into the hallway.

Milbank felt a twinge of pain in his chest as he tried to smooth the wrinkles in his shirt. He then straightened his tie. "Do you need something, Terri?" he said as calmly as he could, trying to ignore everything that had just happened. *She was just a foolish child. This was no big deal.*

Terri cleared her throat. "Excuse me, Governor. Mrs. Milbank is here."

The governor's wife stepped through the doorway.

Chapter 41

Tom sat in a darkened corner of the Blue Clover Café, a trendy bistro tucked away on the second floor of a classic brick building in New London. Two glasses of wine stood on the tabletop between him and his daughter. She was working her way through an Asian pear salad while he nibbled at his cheeseburger. But his second glass of wine was emptier than her first.

They had discovered this place a few weeks ago and liked it so much they had returned twice since. Tonight, he wished he would never have to leave.

While she ate her salad, she talked with excitement about her classes, her great friends in the environmental club—she had been elected secretary—and her quirky roommate. He loved her energy and enthusiasm, the way she gushed about the simple joys of college life.

But he was struggling to find joy. He was in trouble. Deep trouble. If he didn't find a way out, this carefree scene might never be repeated.

"You look distracted," she said. "Is everything okay?"

He snapped out of his trance and forced a smile. "Yeah, of course. Some work stuff on my mind. Tell me more about that oceanography class," he said, grasping at a topic, any topic, to distract him from his thoughts.

She placed her hand over his. "I don't mind hearing about your work."

He had already dumped enough garbage on her for one lifetime, most of it during the death spiral of his marriage to her mother. His eyes misted over. She was a special girl. He mourned the years of her life he had missed out on. "I've just got some trouble at work, but I can handle it. Let's not waste our time talking about that."

She grimaced and pulled her hand back. "Okay, but you look really worried. It's starting to freak me out."

He shook his head. "I don't mean to worry you. I think everything will be fine. I really do. But if not..." He stopped himself just a few words too late.

Her mouth dropped open. She reached out and grabbed his hand. "Dad, please." She squeezed his hand. "What's going on? Is everything okay?"

"It's just some money trouble."

"Oh." She seemed relieved by that response, as well as not particularly surprised. "I bet Mom would help you," she said, her tone far calmer.

The idea wasn't crazy. Tom's ex-wife probably would help him, not that he deserved her help. But that wasn't an option. Not this time. This was too big a hole for his wealthy ex to pull him out of.

"I've got it. I really do." Tom then forced the conversation away from his troubles and back to her studies and extracurricular activities. He even caught a passing reference to a boy.

"We're just friends," she said, blushing and avoiding eye contact.

After they finished their meal, he paid the check. They strolled to the car, drove back to campus, and then a lump formed in his throat as they reached the front of her dorm.

"Goodnight," he said as she took off her seatbelt.

"Goodnight, Dad. Thanks for dinner."

"You're welcome. You know, you're the best thing that ever happened to me."

Even in the dim light, he could see her grin. "Where's that coming from?"

He looked into her eyes. "I just want you to know that."

She planted a kiss on the side of his face then left the car and walked the ten paces to the doorway of Branford House. "I love you," she called back to him.

"I love you too."

He watched as she let herself inside then closed the ornate door behind her. Tears filled his eyes as he clutched the steering wheel.

After a few deep breaths, he started the car again and pulled away from the curb. He needed to turn his luck around. He had to get out of the hole. And there was only one way for him to do so.

He headed toward the casino.

Chapter 42

Jack and Amanda sat at their kitchen table with a series of white take-out containers lined up between them. Jack reached for the one containing chicken and broccoli and pushed a small forkful onto his plate.

"You want some of this?" he asked as he used his thumb to nudge a stray piece of broccoli back into the flimsy box.

"Just a little," she said, sliding her plate in front of him. "I'm not really hungry."

Jack served up a modest helping of food and slid the dish back in front of his wife. He then started picking at his own meal. Efforts at small talk over dinner had largely fizzled out, and they sat in an awkward silence, both knowing they were simply waiting.

Dr. Cunningham had said, "Two or three days." Today was the third.

As they both poked at their food, her cell phone buzzed, rattling against the tabletop.

She grabbed it and hurriedly placed it to her ear. "Hello." Amanda listened intently for a moment then let out a deep breath. "Right, right." Pause. "Okay." A broad smile crossed her face.

Jack exhaled sharply, not realizing that he, too, had been holding his breath. He felt his lips relax into an involuntary smile, his facial expression now matching that of his wife.

"Yeah, I do," Amanda continued. She bit her lip as a tear rolled down one cheek. She sniffed then smiled again. "Are you one hundred percent sure?" After a brief pause and another shed tear, Amanda said, "Thanks so much for calling right away. The wait was killing me." She looked at Jack. "And Jack too." She set the phone back on the tabletop, a smile now permanently plastered on her face. "Everything is fine! The baby is great. No issues at all."

"That's great news." Jack stood from the table, wrapped her in a big hug, and kissed the top of her head. He used his sleeve to wipe a tear off her cheek. "I was a bit worried," he conceded in an epic understatement. He pressed a hand on her belly. They kissed again, more passionately this time.

When they returned to their dinners, their appetites had returned, and they made much quicker work of the food. The conversation resumed, a heavy weight having been lifted from both of them.

On the baby monitor, Nate cried out. They waited in silence. A moment later, they heard him again.

"Bad dream?" Jack asked.

"Probably. I should check." Amanda wiped her mouth with a napkin.

"You want me to go?"

"No, I've got it. You can clean up. Then maybe find a movie?"

"Sounds like a plan." Jack started stacking the dirty dishes.

Amanda stood and took a step toward the nursery. "Oh, by the way," she said as she turned and flashed him a devilish grin. "There's something else you should know."

He froze with a fork in his hand. "What's that?"

"Just some news," she said impishly, toying with him and clearly enjoying it. "Something you might find interesting."

"Come on, Amanda. Spit it out."

She grinned again. "It's a girl."

Chapter 43

Tom chuckled when he spotted a familiar sight across the casino floor. He weaved his way past a couple of rows of tables then took a seat in front of his favorite blond Rhode Islander.

He dropped fifty thousand dollars' worth of chips on the green felt. "You had better not clean me out again."

"Wow," she said as she eyed the stack of chips. "Did I clean you out before?"

"Completely."

"Well then, I owe you. Maybe this is your lucky night."

So far, it had been. After some quick early losses, he had vaulted himself into a fifteen-thousand-dollar gain. Emboldened by the good fortune, he had drawn down his home equity loan and opened a casino line of credit large enough to keep him at the table as long as the cards kept falling his way.

The rational side of his brain had tried to convince him that he was being a fool. No casino run would be large enough to generate the kind of money he needed to repay the Heller estate. And even if he did somehow manage to ride a streak that would make that much cash, he couldn't simply drop the missing funds back in the account and ask Jack to look the other way. But a couple of gin and tonics had made him a bit more optimistic. Jack apparently only knew about a half million of the shortfall. Maybe that was all Tom needed to come up with. And seeing his favorite dealer certainly seemed like a good omen. Miss Rhode Island really did owe him a run of luck. Maybe she would help him find his way out.

He slid a green chip into the circle in front of him to make a bet of five thousand dollars, the table maximum.

The dealer called the oversized bet aloud, attracting the attention of a tuxedo-clad pit boss standing behind her.

"Welcome, sir," the pit boss said, looking at Tom like a fox eying a chicken. "If you need anything tonight, just let us know." He motioned to someone across the room then grinned at Tom before walking away.

The dealer dropped a pair of queens on the felt in front of him. "You *are* lucky tonight. I can feel it."

"I could use some luck. More than ever."

A waitress appeared over his shoulder. "Can I get you something, hon? A cocktail?"

He licked his parched lips. Her timing was impeccable. *Just one more.* "Please. A gin and tonic."

As the dealer slid the next sets of cards onto the table, Tom's premonition seemed to be coming true. His roll continued with hands of twenty, nineteen, and twenty again. His fifty thousand soon turned to eighty, an impressive stack of chips accumulating in front of him. *Yeah, this is my lucky night.*

Over the next two hours, Tom wagered the table maximum on every hand, going up nearly one hundred ninety thousand dollars before slipping back to one hundred twenty thousand. The gin and tonics flowed generously. He was told a hotel suite was waiting for him once he was done at the tables.

He was having a very good night, but the table limits were keeping him from maximizing his good fortune. The stack of chips in front of him was still not nearly what he needed, not even close.

The sportsbook was his only real hope. The limits there were higher, the payouts far greater. He looked at his watch. The west coast games had barely started. Plenty of time to play.

He tossed a five-hundred-dollar chip on the table for the dealer then headed to the cashier window to see what he could do to raise the stakes.

KYLE SAT BEHIND THE wheel of a nondescript black sedan recently confiscated in a drug bust. He drove down Tom's street for the third time in an hour, slowing as he passed Tom's house so he could scan the windows, which stubbornly remained completely dark. He checked his phone again. Still no activity on Tom's cell. *Where the hell is this guy?*

Chapter 44

Daniel Milbank steeled himself as he closed the front door behind him.

Cindy had pulled away from his touches all evening, flashing forced smiles and biting her lip. But in the silence of their privacy, the fury she had masked all night erupted into full display as she slammed their keys on the foyer table before kicking her shoes across the marble floor.

This is about to get ugly. He turned to face her. She was already halfway up the staircase.

"Cindy," he called, "come on, darling."

"Darling?" she scoffed as she continued her ascent without looking back. "Don't even."

Oh, give me a break. He moved toward the stairs. Apparently, he had to chase her like a schoolgirl. "That was not what it seemed. Nothing happened."

When he reached the top step, she was waiting for him with her arms folded across her chest. Her nostrils flared. He'd expected tears and vulnerability. He had seen that before and knew exactly how to manage it. He'd never seen her look so angry with him.

"You disgust me," she snapped. "That was humiliating. *Everyone* saw it."

He took a slow breath. He hadn't been in love with his wife for many years, but he still *appreciated* her. He still understood the role she played in his life. He still knew that nothing he had attained would have been possible without her sacrifice and support. She'd stood beside him through thick and thin, turning an empathetic eye to his faults and a blind eye to his dalliances. He knew today had been humiliating for her, but she needed her to move on, to dig deeper. There was a campaign to wage. This was all a distraction.

He reached out to stroke her cheek. "I'm sorry."

She grabbed the fabric of his suit and pushed his arm away from her. "Don't you dare."

He took a step back, his heart quickening as he teetered on the top step. He grabbed the staircase post to steady himself. "I know you're angry," he said, taking a big step toward her and away from the edge of the stairs, "but we just need—"

"There is no more *we*." She threw her hands in the air. "I'm done. I'm out."

"Let's just—"

"Danny, listen to me. I'm done with this." She spoke with clinical precision, enunciating each word precisely. She pointed at their bedroom door. "Get your stuff out of *my* room."

"Okay, okay. I will." *Good idea.* It wouldn't be the first time he'd spent the night sleeping in the guest suite. It likely wouldn't be the last. *This would all blow over by morning.*

"And get a lawyer," she added. "I want a divorce."

He froze. "Listen, I'm sorry it got so ugly today. Let's just get through the election and then—"

"No! It's always been *your* time. Always the next event or next election. Now it's *my* time. This is happening, and it's happening *now*. I've already retained Margaret Sylvester."

His blood ran cold. *Margaret Sylvester? The infamous divorce lawyer who craved media attention more than Milbank himself did? The lawyer who relished in scandal?* She was the biggest, baddest name Cindy could possibly have thrown at him. Her practice was devoted solely to giving jilted lovers and forsaken spouses all the revenge they could ever ask for. If Cindy was serious, this could bring everything to a crashing end.

What Sylvester started, the blood-thirsty media would finish. The reporters would find others from Milbank's past willing to come out of the woodwork. More than one woman would tell of her exploits with the married governor. The story would grow and build, throwing off his entire message as he headed toward election. He'd ridden out scandals before but never one like this. This would be insurmountable. This would be the end.

He tasted his dinner again as he thought about it, the acrid blend of steak and red wine creeping up his throat. He eyed his wife, contemplating his next move. Her chest heaved. Her cheeks were beet red, and heat radiated off of her, fueled by her burning contempt. She wasn't kidding this time. She wasn't bluffing.

"I love you," he said, once again reaching out to caress her cheek. "I've always loved you."

She pushed him backward, again causing him to stagger toward the precipice of the staircase. He felt a moment of weightlessness before his hand caught the handrail. As he pulled himself back to safety, she stomped away.

"You disgust me," she called back, as if she hadn't already made that sufficiently clear.

She slammed the bedroom door behind her then threw the lock.

Cindy Milbank had just declared war.

Chapter 45

Kyle heard a faint buzzing sound coming from somewhere in the distance. He tried to ignore it, but it persisted, a relentless, annoying hum. He forced his eyes open and saw nothing but blackness as he clawed his way out of what had been a refreshingly deep sleep.

When he regained his bearings, he fumbled on his nightstand for his phone then squinted at the display. *Jesus, not even four a.m. What the hell does he want?*

With a sigh, he answered, "Good morning, Governor," keeping his tone as cheerful as he could manage. He rolled his tongue around his parched mouth as his eyes involuntarily closed. "Is everything okay, sir?" He knew it wasn't. No good news had ever come from Daniel Milbank's calls to Kyle's burner phone, especially those in the middle of the night.

"Did I wake you up?"

"It's fine, Governor." He swallowed a yawn. "What can I do for you?"

"We've got a huge problem."

Kyle forced himself alert. There were a couple of huge problems looming. Milbank needed to be more specific. Kyle slipped out from beneath the covers and sat at the edge of the bed, the room spinning slightly as he did so. "What is it?"

"Cindy wants a divorce," Milbank spat. "Like right now."

Kyle hadn't expected that one. "Right now? Right before the election? Is she crazy?"

"More like furious. I guess I've really done it this time."

The college girl. Kyle didn't even need to ask. He'd heard about that train wreck, and it was no surprise. He had been in the room many times when Milbank had caressed a shoulder or slipped an unwanted hand around some unsuspecting female's waist. Usually, the recipient would laugh it off. Occasionally, they would meekly protest, at which point the governor would reflexively blame his mother. "She was a hugger," he would say, as if she'd somehow never taught her son the distinction between hugging and harassment. The governor had played with fire too many times. He'd finally been burnt.

"I've never seen her so upset," Milbank said. "She won't listen to me. I've tried. She's done."

"I'm sorry, sir." Kyle wondered when his role had extended to that of family therapist. "What can I do to help?"

"And she knows stuff," Milbank added, ignoring Kyle's question but effectively answering it. "I'm worried about what she might do."

Kyle's pulse quickened. This wasn't therapy; this was work. He flipped on a light, bathing the room in a whiteness that seared his eyes. "You want me to call in some help?"

Milbank sighed. "I don't see another option. Do you?"

"Not really. Parameters?"

"Well, don't hurt her, of course. But send a clear shot across the bow. She should shut her mouth. One stern warning. She will be absolutely silent through the election. Then we can figure it out."

"Got it."

"Nobody touches her," Milbank repeated.

"I understand, sir."

"Thanks."

The line went dead.

Kyle tossed the phone back onto his nightstand and turned off the light. He pulled a pillow over his eyes. He didn't like the way things were going. Not one bit. Danny Milbank was flying closer and closer to the sun. The indiscretions had become more frequent, the violence more widespread: one burned-out community center, one dead lawyer, and now Cindy Milbank en route to an encounter with one of Mike Daly's thugs. More calls on burner phones. More shakedowns.

Kyle had no problem with some of his recent tasks. He knew how the game was played. In this political climate, nobody could rise to the top without playing more than their share of hardball. A little graft was par for the course. Occasional threats were an essential element of politics. But Milbank was suddenly taking things to another level, fueled in part by his raw ambition but made far worse by a lack of discipline.

Jessica Baldwin had always been the level-headed one, the one Kyle could count on to counteract Milbank's worst impulses and tantrums. But she, too, had changed. She was suddenly afraid to get her own hands dirty, so she tried to stay above the fray as she focused on taking her seat on the superior court.

All of that left Kyle increasingly exposed and alone. He owed them both a lot. He knew that. He wouldn't be where he was without everything they had done for him. But their loyalties had been just about repaid, the old scores nearly settled.

Kyle slowed his breathing, trying to restrain his racing mind. Once daylight was here, he would make some phone calls to arrange an ambush for Cindy Milbank. He would yet again do the governor's bidding. He would once more be the one, the only one, who actually got things done.

But first, he needed some more sleep.

Chapter 46

Tom forced his eyes open and let out an involuntary groan. His head pounded with every heartbeat. His tongue felt as if it had been glued to the roof of his mouth. He grabbed a glass off the nightstand and took a long gulp. What he'd expected to be water turned out to be stale gin and lime, causing him to gag.

He got up and stumbled across the room to the windows. He opened the drapes, and bright sunshine poured in, the intense rays burning his eyes and illuminating the wreckage of the night before. His clothes were scattered all over the floor. The living room table was covered with remnants of the steak dinner he'd ordered at midnight, when he'd needed a little nourishment before he went back to the sportsbook in one final effort to recoup his losses. It was all coming back to him.

It hadn't gone well.

Indeed, while the day had started off brilliantly, it had ended with nothing short of carnage. He'd maxed out all his lines of credit, going down a healthy six figures, before a casino manager took him aside to tell him it was time to stop. All the casino could offer was an escort back to his suite and an invitation to stay a couple of extra nights on the house. "A little vacation," they'd called it. "Enjoy," they'd had the audacity to add.

Sleep had come eventually but lasted just a few hours before a heart-pounding nightmare brought him back to an even more unsettling reality.

He grabbed his boxers and socks off the floor, feeling an emptiness in his gut. He slipped on his wrinkled clothes from the night before. He'd done it again. He was heading down the same road, destined to reach the same dead end. This time, there was no way out. At least not alone.

He plucked his cell phone from the nightstand and dialed the number of the only person he thought might be able to help.

"Hello."

"I'm so sorry for all the trouble," Tom choked out. He began to sob.

"It will all be okay," Jack replied, his tone far more gracious than Tom could've expected. "But we really need to talk this through."

Tom swiped at his eyes and steadied his voice. "I know we do. I can be down there in a few hours."

"Where are you?"

"I went to visit my daughter."

"In New London?"

"Yeah. I stayed up this way, but I'm about to head home."

"Good."

"So what do we do?"

"I've got a friend at the FBI. He's the one to talk to. I trust him completely."

Tom's stomach dropped. *The FBI?* The thought filled him with dread. But he had no other choice. "I guess you should call him."

"I already have. I just need to tell him you're ready to talk."

"Do I have a choice?"

"I don't think so."

"All right then. Go ahead and set it up." His whole body was shaking uncontrollably.

"So how big is this thing, Tom?"

"Big."

"How big?"

"I honestly don't really know. I only get to see a tiny piece, this cop I deal with. He's the only player I know for sure. But he's told me there's more and warned me not to go looking for it. I don't know where it ends."

"Do you have records? Anything that will create probable cause?"

"Yeah. There's a clear paper trail—a series of statements."

"Where are they?"

"On my laptop. At home."

"Then go straight there. I'll call my guy at the FBI and get him to send someone over."

Tom reached for his shoes. "Okay."

After a long silence, Jack said, "It will work out."

"I'm sorry." Tom couldn't think of anything else to say. "I'm really sorry."

"I know you are. We can fix it. Just get home. Gather everything, and then we'll figure out the next steps."

"Okay. I'm on my way."

After hanging up, Tom put on his shoes, tidied up the room as best he could, and collected his things. As he headed toward the door, his cell phone buzzed. He brought up his texting app.

Jack: Talked to Joe. He'll get an agent to your house first thing tomorrow Gather all the records.

Tom: Will do. I'm sorry for all of this.

Jack: Just give him everything. It will all be fine.

KYLE'S PHONE PINGED. He pulled it from his pocked and saw the text messages rolling in off Tom's tapped phone. *Shit!* He placed a call to Mike Daly.

"Two times in one day?" Daly said. "You're a busy man."

"Tell me about it. Remember that rodent problem in Greenwich? I need an exterminator, ASAP."

"Can do."

Kyle checked his watch. "Where are you?"

"I can meet you in 30 minutes. The usual spot?"

"Yeah, see you there."

Chapter 47

Tom took a sip from his cup of steaming black tea then sneaked a peek through the shuttered blinds. The backcountry Greenwich sky was darkening, leaving a sole porch lamp standing guard in front of the house. All was quiet as far as he could see.

He was getting ready for what he expected to be the longest night of his life, the final sleepless hours before the FBI arrived in the morning. Everything was all organized on the dining room table: two laptops, a tall stack of papers comprising a complete record of the true paper trail in the Heller estate, and a yellow pad containing handwritten records sufficient to take down Kyle Stone. He was ready. Or at least as ready as he could be.

He was also about ready to vomit. He hadn't eaten since breakfast, and even that had only been half a muffin forced down in little pieces as he drove home from the casino. He had no desire for food, no ability to think of anything other than what sat on his dining room table and what lay ahead of him. He forced down another sip of tea.

He had a sense of what his life would be like in the coming weeks and months. He would be an informant, a rat, trying to lead the FBI from Kyle to whomever he reported to. Even in the best-case scenario, Tom would probably never work again. He would become a pariah, the disgraced attorney who saved his own neck by turning on those around him. He would be the subject of fascination in some corners, scorn and ridicule in others. But even so, cooperating with the FBI was his best way out. No public arrest. No lengthy prison time. A morally ambiguous record of a largely victimless crime.

And if he lived long enough, maybe he could make a run at redemption. Reclaiming his reputation after a period of penance was all he could hope for given the hole he'd dug himself into.

He walked into the pantry and set down his tea. He grabbed a glass out of a cabinet and filled it with bourbon. When he took a swig of the heavily charred liquid, the taste of caramelized sugar filled his mouth before he let it slip down his throat. After another mouthful, he was taken by the stillness of the house around him. All he heard was the hum of the refrigerator in the kitchen and the sound of a dog barking off in the distance.

It will all be okay, Jack had assured him again and again. Tom wasn't at all convinced. All he knew was that the life he had known would be coming to an end. The future was impossible to predict.

He jumped when he saw the glare of a set of headlights cross his lawn. The sound of an engine told him the vehicle was coming up his driveway. A car door slammed. The neighbor's dog barked again.

Who the hell was that? He quickly set down the glass and scurried over to the window. Sliding a finger between two slats of the blinds, he peered out.

A man stepped out of a nondescript sedan and slowly walked up the front path. A pair of oversized glasses reflected the ambient light, obscuring most of the guy's face.

Tom's pulse quickened as the man approached.

Chapter 48

Jack paced across the living room, a baseball bat resting on his shoulder, as the Yankees batted on the muted television. He took a sip of beer then looked at the sofa behind him, watching his wife's chest rise then lower as she slept.

He turned to the TV. After a long fly ball hooked just outside of the foul pole, Jack glanced at the baby monitor on the table next to him and then back at Amanda. Everyone was still fast asleep. All quiet in the house. This was a rare moment in their crazy lives. And it was about to get rarer. The coming months would bring a new baby, a new house, and—Jack shuddered—whatever was going to happen with Tom and CWO. Peace and quiet would be harder to come by. *A lot harder*. But for the moment, the silence was blissful.

He gripped the bat tighter as the Yankee third baseman hit another towering fly ball to the left. Jack loosened his grip once the ball had dropped into the outfielder's mitt. Jack groaned.

Amanda roused, raising her head and turning onto her side. She then sat up, stretching her arms upward as she yawned. "How long was I out?"

"I don't know. Twenty minutes?"

"God, that sofa is uncomfortable," she said, turning her head from side to side.

"I know. We really need to get rid of that."

"Speaking of things we should get rid of...." She pointed at the bat. "Do you really need that?"

"Absolutely. Do *not* mess with the bat." The bat was the latest addition to Jack's eclectic collection of sports memorabilia. His father had acquired it from Yankee Stadium on Bat Day in 1970, and Jack had discovered it a few weeks ago in the attic of his parents' house. The Yankees had won eleven of fifteen games since he'd found the old relic.

"I still can't believe they used to hand out bats to everyone walking into Yankee Stadium," Amanda said.

"I think it was just the kids."

She shook her head. "Whatever. But we should still find a new place for that. The garage maybe?"

"I'll think about it."

She stretched her neck again then lay back down. "You know what I could really go for?" she asked without opening her eyes.

"What?"

"A Blizzard."

"Great idea! Go get us a couple, would you? I'll just sit down and finish my beer."

She groaned.

"Just kidding." He laid the bat on the coffee table. "Oreo or Snickers?"

"Oreo, of course." She smirked. "How long have you known me?"

"Thought you might be feeling adventurous."

She shook her head. "You don't mess with a classic."

"Fine. *I'll* have the Snickers." He walked into the kitchen and put on his shoes. "Hey, mind if I walk to get them? I could use the exercise."

"No problem. I'll just hang here and watch the Yankees. Did they arm the crowd tonight? Because that could get interesting."

He laughed. "I'll be back in twenty minutes."

"Okay, but be careful out there. It's a pretty dark night."

"Don't worry," he replied as he opened the door. "It's not exactly a dangerous neighborhood."

"Maybe take your bat." She chuckled. "Just in case."

Chapter 49

Tom's doorbell rang.

He cringed behind the front door. "Can I help you?" he called.

"This is Special Agent Jackson with Financial Crimes."

Tom looked through the small window that adorned the thick oak slab.

The man outside smiled and displayed a badge. With his scruffy beard, he didn't exactly look the part of a white-collar investigator. "Don't worry," he said with a broad smile. "I'm here to help. Jack's friend sent me."

Tom relaxed at the mention of Jack's name. "I thought you were coming in the morning," he said as he opened the door.

"I thought we'd start early."

"That's nice of you. I wouldn't have slept tonight anyway."

The special agent stepped inside and chuckled. "You look nervous."

"That's an understatement," Tom replied as he shut the door.

"Well, just relax. Everything is going to be okay. Really. Just give me what I need, and you'll be fine."

Tom took a deep breath, perhaps his first of the entire day. "I'm glad you think so. But you're not the one looking at felony charges."

"Don't worry, man. All of this is going to work out. But you've got to work with me, okay?"

"Okay." *What other choice did he have?*

"I've done this before," Jackson said. "If you want to walk away from this, we need to do it right the first time. Tell me everything. Give me all your records. No hedging. No holding back. You do any of that, and a judge is going to make you pay. You'll do years in a rathole prison. You got it?"

The urge to vomit gripped his throat, but Tom swallowed it down. "I do."

"Good. You got someplace comfortable we can sit?"

"Yeah. Come in here." Tom led Jackson into the dining room. He pointed at his laptop on the table. "Everything is in there."

Jackson sat at the head of the table and pulled the laptop in front of him. He pointed at the chair next to him. "Have a seat."

After Tom complied, Jackson took out a pen and note pad then flashed another toothy smile. "So, let's start at the beginning. Tell me what's happened with your law firm. Who there knows about this?"

Tom thought that seemed like an odd place to start, but he figured the agent knew what he was doing. "My partner cornered me and told me he had figured out what was going on."

The agent scribbled furiously. "Which partner? What's his name?"

"Jack Collins."

"Anyone else?"

Tom shook his head. "I don't think so."

"You *don't think so*?" The agent slapped the table. "Are you holding out on me?"

Tom's stomach flipped. "I haven't told anyone else. I'm sure Jack didn't either."

"Okay, go on. What does Jack know? Did you give him any names?"

Something was wrong. This guy should be asking about the money, about Kyle, about the wires. But he wasn't. It was almost as if he already knew all of that. *Oh, shit.* A wave of nausea overcame him as he broke out into a cold sweat.

Jackson raised one eyebrow. "You okay?"

"Yeah, I'm just so nervous about all of this." Tom wiped some sweat from his forehead. His mind spun as he tried to figure out what he should say. "Let me try to focus here. Jack really doesn't know anything. He just knows that the account doesn't balance. He thinks I took some money. As far as he knows, I was working alone."

"So he doesn't know any details?"

"No. I've covered my trail pretty well. He'll never put it all together."

"Okay. So let's shift gears." Jackson placed his hand on the laptop. "Everything is on here, right?"

"Yeah."

"Any backups?"

"No."

"You sure?"

"Completely. It's all on my personal laptop. The firm doesn't even know about it." This guy wasn't here to help, at least not to help Tom.

"Any copies anywhere else?" Jackson asked.

"No, that's it."

"You sure?"

"Yes."

"Where's your phone?" Jackson's tone was growing more aggressive.

"I don't know what's going on here, but this isn't—"

Jackson got up and stood beside Tom. He slid open his jacket to reveal a holstered gun. "You really screwed up, buddy." He placed a hand on Tom's shoulder and squeezed. "You made a real mess. I'm here to clean it up."

Tom gulped. "Who are you?"

"You said you've got a daughter, right? Where does she go to school?"

"Chicago," Tom replied, quite certain that he hadn't mentioned his daughter.

Jackson—Tom felt certain that was not the man's real name—leaned over until his face was uncomfortably close. The smell of second-hand pot wafted up Tom's nose. When Tom tried to lean away, Jackson pushed down on his shoulder, holding him in place.

"Now you see," Jackson snarled, "that's exactly the kind of shit I don't need. You think you're dealing with an amateur? Branford House, room 208. Pretty girl. Nice room. Easy access through a window."

The room began to spin. Tom turned his head and vomited onto the rug. The guy removed his hand, and Tom lurched, nearly falling into the mess.

"Whoa! Easy there, buddy." The fake agent grabbed Tom by his collar and straightened him in his chair. "You need some water?"

Tom wiped his mouth with his sleeve. "No."

"Okay, let's try this again. And this time, no messing around. We don't want anyone getting hurt, right?"

"Please don't hurt my daughter," Tom said, already certain *he* was not going to survive this encounter. "She knows nothing about this."

"She'll be just fine. You got a phone?" Jackson asked.

"Right here," Tom said, pulling his cell out of his pocket.

"Good. Give it to me."

Tom's hand shook as he handed over his phone.

"You got another?" Jackson asked.

"No."

"No *burner*?"

"No."

"Okay." Jackson sat back down and opened the laptop. "Now let's go through all this stuff. We've got a lot of work to do tonight."

Chapter 50

As Jack pulled into Tom's driveway, he spotted the silver Ford parked in front of the garage. The driver was leaning against the car and talking on his phone. He was dressed in a white shirt and drab gray suit and tie, with his close-cropped salt-and-pepper hair completing the monochromatic look. Even if Jack hadn't known the guy was FBI, he would have pegged him for a Fed.

Jack cut the engine and got out of his car.

The man slipped his phone into his pocket and stepped forward. "Victor Simonte." He squinted into the morning light and extended his hand. "Thanks for coming over so quickly."

"Nice to meet you, Agent Simonte," Jack said. "Thanks for the heads up."

Simonte nodded. "Glad to do it, but I'm not sure what we can do here. Everything's locked up tight. Without a warrant, I can't do more." The agent had told Jack as much when he called him but graciously agreed to wait while Jack drove over to help sort things out.

"That's weird," Jack said. "I talked to him yesterday. He knew you were coming this morning."

Jack walked over to the garage and peered in the windows. Tom's blue Bentley was safely tucked inside, along with the far more practical Subaru he drove only when winter weather forced his hand.

"His cars are here," Jack reported as he dialed Tom's number yet again. The call rang several times then went to voicemail. "Let me walk around back."

"Sure."

Jack walked from the driveway onto the rear lawn and circled the house. Looking up at the grey clapboard, he could see ambient light through most of the windows on the top floor. Yet Tom's bedroom remained dark. Jack cupped his hands around his mouth and yelled up at the blackened windows. "Tom! Wake up!"

He waited a few seconds but saw no movement. He walked closer to the house and peered through the living room blinds. The place was pristine, exactly how it had looked the last time he'd visited.

Jack stepped off the grass and slid his leg between two small shrubs planted against the foundation. He slipped through them and looked into Tom's office window. Nothing seemed amiss, at least nothing he could see in the sliver of light coming in through the doorway. The desk was cleared of papers. The chair was tucked neatly in place.

He raised his hands to shield his eyes from glare as he pressed his face against the glass. His breath caught as he saw something on the floor, jutting out from behind the desk. *Is that a leg? Shit.*

He banged on the window. "Tom!" He reached out and tried to open the window, but it didn't budge.

"Agent Simonte!" Jack called out toward the front yard. "Come back here."

Jack sprang out from amid the foundation plantings and scoured the ground. Simonte appeared just as Jack lifted a fist-sized rock from the mulch.

"What the hell is going on?" Simonte asked.

"I see something on the floor in there. I think it's Tom." Jack threw the rock at the window, shattering the glass. He picked up another rock and used it to clear out more of the pane before reaching through to flip the lock.

Simonte yelped. "Jesus! What the hell are you doing?"

"I'm going in." Jack lifted the sash then tore off his jacket and laid it over the sill. He gingerly climbed through the opening, trying to avoid any remaining shards of glass.

Once inside, Jack rushed around the desk and knelt beside the man lying on the floor. When he rolled the body over, he gasped. *Tom!*

Jack placed his ear against Tom's chest. No heartbeat. He grabbed Tom's wrist. The skin was cold. Jack's fingers rubbed against Tom's watchband as he vainly searched for a pulse.

Simonte joined him on the floor. "Is this Tom?"

"Yeah." Jack sat back on his haunches and wiped his eyes.

"I'll take over here. You go call an ambulance." Simonte pressed two fingers against Tom's neck then leaned over to put his ear to Tom's mouth. "And unlock the door for the paramedics."

Jack whipped out his phone and dialed 911.

"I need an ambulance," Jack said as he paced the living room, his heart pounding. "I'm at 42 Richardson Lane. Off Lake Avenue."

"What's the emergency?"

"It's my law partner. He's unresponsive on the floor."

"I've got an ambulance on the way. Are there any injuries? Any idea what happened?"

"None at all. I just found him on the floor."

As he answered a few final questions from the dispatcher, Jack raced to the front door as Simonte had instructed him to do. He flipped the deadbolt, flung open the door, then ran back to Tom's office.

Simonte stood behind the desk, taking photos of the contents. "I'm sorry," he said as Jack entered the room. "He's gone. Maybe head out front to meet the paramedics?"

"Can I have a minute here?"

"Just a minute. And don't touch anything." Simonte stood and touched Jack's shoulder before stepping away.

Jack slipped to the floor and sat beside his former partner. Dressed in one of his usual crisp white shirts, the departed Tom was a slighter, paler version of the living one that Jack had seen just two days ago. He remembered Tom, angry and scared, bolting from the office. That would be the last time Jack saw him. Jack knew he would carry that final painful memory with him for the rest of his life.

A faint siren blared in the distance. Minutes later, tires crunched on the gravel driveway.

"Back here!" Simonte yelled. Moments later, an EMT brushed past him to enter the room.

The paramedic dropped his bag and knelt beside Tom. He began his own search for a pulse then put a stethoscope to Tom's chest. After only a few moments, he shook his head. "Nothing," he said. "I'm sorry."

"Let's clear out," Simonte told Jack as the EMT picked up his gear. "I'm going to call in the locals. Why don't you go outside for some air?"

Jack climbed to his feet. Tears welled up in his eyes. He sniffed in deeply as he took one final glance at his departed law partner. Turning away, he wiped his nose against his sleeve.

His sleeve. He spun around and stared down at Tom again. His stomach dropped.

Jack bent over and slid Tom's shirt sleeve up, revealing the plain black band he remembered touching earlier. He turned over the wrist and eyed the square gold watch face. The name Lange was clearly visible on the dial.

Holy shit!

Chapter 51

Jessica Baldwin leaned against the wooden railing and looked out at the horizon. A line of puffy clouds slid across the sapphire-blue sky. The Mianus River rushed by just beyond the trees, yesterday's rainfall splashing and gurgling its way downstream. The bottle of wine on the table beside her was nearly empty, as was the plate of cheese and crackers, which she realized in retrospect had been too small to soak up all the alcohol.

She took another celebratory sip, reflecting on the pieces of her plan that were neatly falling into place. Her superior court appointment was assured. Danny's reelection appeared increasingly likely. Even Tom's suicide had nicely wrapped up another loose end, a sentiment Jessica had skillfully hidden from the throngs of lawyers she'd chatted with at his funeral earlier that morning. Everything was working out, with one glaring exception.

She looked over at Kyle, who was staring out at the river while nursing the same beer he'd opened when she'd uncorked the bottle of wine. He had taken small sips. He had offered smatterings of conversation.

For weeks, ever since he'd found out about her looming appointment to the superior court, he'd been increasingly short-tempered and detached, turning down at least three offers of dinner before accepting this one. Even today, this was an angry version of Kyle.

"Cindy's making a lot of noise," he muttered out of the blue.

Her chest tightened. "Does she know?"

"No, no... not about you. But... well, you know... there's other stuff."

She did know about the "other stuff." She tried to ignore it. "So what's going on?"

"I think she's really going to leave him this time."

Her heart fluttered. "Really?"

"Yeah. We'll hold her off until after the election, but beyond that, who knows?" He shrugged.

The word "election" refocused her tipsy brain. What she personally found welcome news actually brought a far more complicated issue. A divorce would seriously delay, if not completely derail, Milbank's aspirations for the future. A recently divorced person certainly *could* run for Senate, but he might decide not to risk the scandal. Cindy knew far too much. If the press pestered her enough, or if she got a thirst for revenge, the reporters might eventually get their story.

Thinking hurt her brain as she tried to process the possibilities. Danny's upward path would hit a snag, their carefully laid plans derailed by a premature divorce. But he'd be free. *Finally.* She might end up standing by his side rather than being whisked to and fro in freight elevators and under cover of darkness. Plus, if he deferred the Senate run, he might stay governor long enough to elevate her to the Appellate Court. She might end up with *everything.*

Of course, she had her own impediment to that happily-ever-after. Andrew Stern was a loyal, supportive husband. He was a good man, a faithful provider. But if Daniel Milbank ever became available, she wouldn't hesitate to leave Andrew for him. Not for an instant.

"What are you thinking?" Kyle asked.

"I'm thinking maybe everything is falling into place."

"Oh yeah? You actually *want* Cindy Milbank going off the deep end?"

Jessica yielded to the alcohol and closed her eyes. The darkness swirled around her as she struggled to keep her balance. "I just want her to keep her mouth shut," she said. "As long as she does that, she can go wherever the hell she wants."

Chapter 52

Daniel Milbank leaned back in his chair, his shoes resting on his desk and his phone pressed against his ear. On the other end of the line was the governor of New York.

Milbank had developed an excellent working relationship with Governor John Stack and an even better friendship. The youngest governor in New York history, Stack's reputation for drinking and carousing was seen as a sign of youthful vigor in the bachelor politician, as were the throngs of women who always seemed to surround him. Milbank took every opportunity he could to spend time with his counterpart from the Empire State, vicariously reliving the days when he, too, had been young and unattached.

"How about we go hunting soon?" Milbank asked. "Maybe the Adirondacks for bear?"

"Absolutely. I can get my family cabin in Jay anytime you like. I'd be glad to have you as my guest."

"Sounds great. We'll get the schedulers to work something out. I'm thinking maybe the end of the month, if that works for you. I'd love to—"

Milbank's door suddenly flew open. What seemed like his entire protective detail quickly filled the room. One agent stepped over to the windows, closed the blinds, and drew the drapes. Another took the phone from Milbank's hand and dismissed Governor Stack with a quick apology.

Milbank glared at the trooper in charge. "What the hell is going on?"

"Governor, there's been an incident," Lieutenant Sharon Duncan said. Her chest heaved as she spoke, and her forehead glistened with sweat. "A break-in at your home."

His jaw fell slack. A wave of adrenaline coursed through his veins. This was much more emotional than he had expected, far more intense than he had imagined it would be.

"Was anyone hurt?"

"Mrs. Milbank was confronted, sir. I don't think she was injured, but paramedics are on the scene. We've got the car coming around to take you home."

Sweat poured from his armpits. A wave of nausea overtook him, causing the room to spin. "Yes, let's go."

An unseen set of arms helped him from his chair.

"We'll get a full briefing in the car," Duncan said. "What we know so far is that a single male entered the residence. We believe he was armed. He engaged with Mrs. Milbank and then fled."

The governor's knees buckled as he grasped the reality of what he had unleashed upon his wife. *She must have been terrified. They better not have hurt her.*

"Are you okay, sir?" Duncan asked.

"I'm fine."

"The car is ready," another trooper reported.

"Okay, let's go," Milbank said. He moved away from the desk, his legs now fully steady beneath him.

The officers formed a tight formation as they led him out of his office and down the stairway. They eventually emerged through the Capitol basement and into his waiting car. Given the fear he was experiencing, he could only imagine what must be running through their heads. An unknown gunman. *Could there be others? Could they be coming after Milbank?*

Duncan guided the governor into his waiting car, then hopped in beside him.

"Go," she shouted to the driver. She fastened her seatbelt then turned to the governor. "We've got mostly Greenwich local on the scene, but troopers are on their way. Your security cameras got a good photo of the suspect. We're running it now."

Yeah, good luck with that. Milbank wondered what fate Mike Daly had arranged for the unknown assailant. He was probably already dead in the back of someone's car.

As the SUV raced through downtown Hartford, Milbank struggled to force oxygen into his quivering lungs. Flashing lights surrounded them as they merged onto the highway, the increasing speed pressing Milbank firmly against the back of his seat. The nausea was back. He popped a mint into his mouth.

He looked into the rear-view mirror and eyed the driver. Even though they were hurtling down the highway at ninety miles an hour, Kyle hadn't even broken a sweat. His features were slack. He calmly chewed a wad of gum. Just another day at the office.

Milbank didn't know if the man was simply that well trained or just pathological. Either way, the governor was glad to have him in the driver's seat, literally and figuratively.

As if sensing Milbank's stare, Kyle looked back over his shoulder. "Don't worry, Governor," he said with an eerie calmness. "I've got everything under control."

Chapter 53

Jessica Baldwin kept the gas pedal pressed to the floor as she raced down Merritt Parkway. She slapped at the display, turning off the news report that had just so infuriated her.

Stupid, bumbling idiots. Klutzy, heavy-handed morons.

She put her phone on speaker and dialed Kyle's cell.

"Hello, Jess—"

"Was that your dumb idea or his?"

"Hey, hey, hold on. What are you talking about?"

"Don't give me that. Your little stunt with Cindy Milbank. You think that's not obvious to the entire world?"

"I don't know what you're talking about. And if I did, I'd say no, it's not obvious. Things happen. People break into houses. All the time, in fact."

"Breaking into a woman's house?" Jessica had a rare moment of empathy. *The woman must have been terrified.* "When did we decide to play things that way?"

"He authorized it."

"Well, *he* doesn't always think things through. So that's what I'm supposed to do. Did anyone actually have a plan here, actually consider how this is going to play out?"

"Yeah, we did. She shuts her mouth for a few more weeks. Your beau wins his election. You get your promotion. And by the way, I get shit, as usual. *That's* how this is going to play out. So what's the problem?"

"The *problem* is that nobody talked to me about this." *How dare they do something like this without letting her know? How dare they disrespect her by keeping her out of the loop?*

"We didn't need your input."

"My *input*? You damn well need my *input*." She slapped the steering wheel. "On *everything*. I don't know who you think you are, but you're forgetting your place. You're not running this operation, *Sergeant*. And neither is *he*."

He laughed dismissively. "Actually, I mentioned it to you the other afternoon. I said we'd hold her off. I seem to recall your saying you just wanted her to keep her mouth shut. So you got exactly what you asked for."

"We did not talk about *this*."

"Maybe you were a bit too sauced to remember."

"Screw you."

"Whatever. I don't know what's gotten into you here, but trust me—it's all fine. She's sitting home, nice and quiet. Just like *you* wanted. Nobody got hurt. And he's untouchable now. A nice little public-sympathy bounce, and nobody's going to throw a punch at him right now. It was a brilliant play. Even without your blessed input."

She couldn't fault his reasoning. But the process was still all wrong. She had earned a seat at the table, at the head of it, in fact. All of this had been her plan from the start. They didn't dare forget that.

But butting heads with Kyle would get her nowhere. She mentally counted to five and willed her body to relax. "Listen. Just no more freelancing. I'm in on all the planning from now on."

"Yes, ma'am. I understand."

"Good, thank you," she said as politely as she could then ended the call.

Chapter 54

Daniel Milbank strode into the living room, Sharon Duncan right behind him. His wife sat slumped on the sofa, a nearly empty glass of red wine perched on the table beside her. Her hair fell sloppily around her face, her weekly four-hundred-dollar cut and color an uncharacteristically tousled mess. A streak of mascara arched down from her left eye and across her cheek. She sat in stony silence as they approached, seemingly unaware that they were even in the house. Clearly, she'd had more than one glass.

The governor touched the side of her face. "Cindy. Are you okay?"

"I'm fine," she slurred, recoiling from his hand. She turned her bloodshot eyes toward the female trooper. "The guy didn't touch me. Nothing to worry about."

Duncan bent down and hugged her. "I'm so glad you're safe. I'm so sorry."

Although nominally in charge of the governor's security, Duncan had always expressed concern for the whole Milbank family. While she could neither have foreseen nor prevented the events of the day, she undoubtedly considered them a black mark on her own record.

"I think we're all set," the governor said. "The local car out front is sufficient." he added, referencing the Greenwich police cruiser sitting in the Milbanks' driveway. "You and the team can call it a day."

"I'm not sure one unit in the driveway is enough," Duncan said. "I can stay."

Milbank headed back to the door. "No, no. It's fine. We're fine." He put a hand on the doorknob. "Really. You can go."

Duncan relented and left.

As the front door closed behind the trooper, Cindy Milbank's energy returned, and her placid demeanor disappeared. "You bastard," she hissed through gritted wine-stained teeth. "You are a real piece of work."

"Nobody touched you, right? They promised me."

She rose from the sofa, getting nearly to her feet before falling back onto the cushion. Her arm bumped the glass of wine on the end table, sending it tumbling onto the oriental rug.

He extended a hand to help her up.

"Don't," she snapped. "Don't you dare touch me. Ever."

He stepped back, his hands in the air. "This is not forever," he said. "I just need—"

"You need? *Want.* You *want.* After all these years, you go thug on me? Sending a punk here to give me a talking to? Like I'm just someone else you need to steamroll?"

"Cindy, you need to—"

"You win, okay? You win. That's what you wanted to hear. I'll play it your way. I will keep my mouth shut and bide my time. But I will *hate* you for every minute of my life."

The words hit him hard. He had indeed trapped his wife in a marriage she despised, made her a prisoner of his political ambition. He hated having to do it. He hated what they had become. But he didn't have another option. And it wasn't all his fault. *She* was the one who'd made the veiled threats. *She* was the one who was getting ready for a bare-knuckles divorce, trading silence for an extortive settlement. She'd forced his hand. *He'd had no choice.*

"You forced me into this," he said. "You gave me no other choice."

She finally managed to get to her feet, and she stumbled past him. "You're a bastard," she called over her shoulder as she reached the staircase.

A minute later, a door slammed on the second floor.

He walked into the kitchen and snatched a wine glass from the cabinet. He filled it with the little bit that remained in the open bottle of merlot sitting on the counter. He moved to the kitchen windows and stared out into the backyard.

She was right. He was a bastard. He had been a lousy husband for over a decade, pursuing his own ambitions and expecting, even demanding, that she find happiness in being a politician's wife. For a while, it seemed she had. She did her charity work. She supported his appearances. She focused on family. But times had changed. Their children had left the nest. Their passion had long since dried up. There was no new chapter for them to write together.

But whatever she might want, she needed to be reasonable. This was not the time for a divorce. The illusion of their happy family had to be maintained, at least for now. Someday, she would get her way. Once he was in the Senate, they could amicably split, when the election was in the past and the advisors said the time was right. Until then, she would do what the stranger who'd stood in this kitchen just a few hours earlier had undoubtedly told her to do: keep smiling, shut her mouth, and make no threats or demands. If she did all of that, she would be fine. If she didn't, the next visit wouldn't end nearly as well.

Milbank wasn't sure he could ever actually follow through on those threats. As it was, he'd made Kyle promise repeatedly that she wouldn't be hurt. But he imagined she would never take that chance, never back her husband so deep into a corner that the only way out would be right through her.

He took a hearty swallow of wine, the warm velvet flowing down his throat.

She'd given him no other choice.

Chapter 55

Jack stepped into the lobby of Maplewood Gardens. The scent of lilies nearly overpowered him as he approached the front desk. Beside a massive display of flowers, Robert Granville was waiting for him.

"That's an impressive display," Jack said as he shook Granville's hand.

"We have a ninetieth birthday party this afternoon. The grandchildren went a little overboard.

"I'll say. Anyway, you've got me awfully curious about Mrs. Heller. What's going on?"

"Sorry for the mystery," the director said. "But you should see this for yourself. Trust me. It will be worth the trip."

Granville then led him briskly down the main hallway, nodding and smiling as he went but skipping his usual glad-handing of the residents. He stopped only once they had entered one of the lounges. Across the room, beneath a large window, a group of four ladies sat around a table, Sarah Heller among them. As he stepped up to them, he noticed the tabletop covered with dominos, an interconnected mess of mismatched tiles, at least a few of which were upside down.

Sarah Heller added a random tile to the mix. "How's that move?" she asked as she slid a five up against a six.

The others enthusiastically complimented her, all agreeing that she had made an excellent play.

The director approached a seating area where a television played the local news in front of an empty sofa, the sound blaring at an unhealthy volume. He tapped the remote several times, bringing the booming newscast down to a more reasonable level. He then swiped something off the coffee table and dramatically waved it in the air.

"This week's *Connecticut Record*." He held up the weekly newspaper and asked Jack, "Have you read it?"

"Not yet. Anything good?"

"A nice photo of the governor." Granville smiled awkwardly.

"Seriously, what's going on?"

"Sorry. I'll cut to the chase."

Granville leafed through the paper then settled on a specific page and folded it in half. He handed it to Jack. "Take a look at the photo."

The picture was of the governor presenting an award to a state trooper.

Jack scanned the photo. "What am I looking at?"

"Watch this." Granville marched over to the ladies' table and slipped the photo atop the dominoes in front of Sarah Heller.

"That again?" she growled, swatting at the air with the back of her hand.

"I thought you could tell Mr. Collins what you told me," Granville suggested.

"I don't want to keep talking about this. It's a bad memory. Please." She made another shooing motion. "Take that away."

"I'm sorry to bother you with this, Mrs. Heller, but would you mind just telling me one more time? I think it might be very helpful for Mr. Collins to hear."

"Fine," she huffed. "That's the man who was at my home the morning Sam died." She turned her attention back to the pile of dominoes.

"The governor?" Jack asked, his pulse pounding.

"No, not him," she scoffed as if Jack had already heard this story a dozen times. "The general standing next to him. I bet he's the one who took the watch. All he could talk about was the money, the money." She glared at Granville. "I've told you this all before."

"A general?" Jack cocked his head.

"You mean the one in the blue uniform?" Granville offered. "The state trooper."

"Yes, that's the one." She crossed her arms. "How many times do I need to repeat myself? He and Tom were together in Sam's room. I've told you this so many times."

"He was there?" Jack asked. "A state trooper?"

"That man," Sarah tapped a bony finger on the trooper's face. "That's all I can tell you. Now really, gentlemen, may I get back to my game?"

Stunned, Jack looked up at Granville. "Wow."

The director nodded back. He said nothing, but his message was crystal clear. *I told you so.*

Chapter 56

Internally, they referred to the speech as "the hard line." A duo of speechwriters had needed just a few hours to pull it together after Cindy Milbank had stared down an intruder in her own kitchen. It would mark a sharp pivot in the governor's rhetoric, making him appear even tougher on crime while at the same time ever more committed to restoring some of Connecticut's more blighted cities. Compassionate, yet resolute.

This would not be the first time Milbank had spoken in the wake of tragedy. His administration had borne witness to its share of horrific accidents, more than one mass shooting, and even a rogue October hurricane. Even though this time the tragedy was far more personal, Milbank's goal in responding remained the same. He would not exploit what had happened but rather look beyond it, his eyes and rhetoric focused on the brighter future ahead for himself and his state. It was a tap dance he had come to master.

Hidden around the corner of the building, Milbank could hear the rumble of the crowd. They were ready. And so was he. "Okay," Milbank said to Terri. He took a final swig from a bottle of water before handing it to her. "It's time."

"Go get 'em." She gestured at the troopers poised ready to clear Milbank's path to the stage.

Milbank's heart rate cranked up as he strode out of the shadows of the early autumn evening and approached the white spotlights bathing the steps of Greenwich Town Hall. Tiny wavelets of applause broke out as the first few noticed his entourage on the move, the volume ascending as more and more people joined in. By the time he reached the podium, the crowd had erupted into a deafening roar. Applause and whistles echoed off the stately brick facade as he waved and nodded at his boisterous supporters.

Milbank cleared his throat and fiddled with the half-dozen microphones set out in front of him. "Thank you so much. Thank you for the outpouring of love and support, the good wishes that have meant so much to me and my family in a very difficult time."

The crowd started clapping and hooting again.

"Thank you all!" Milbank boomed as the applause began to drown him out.

He looked out into the sea of faces. They covered the entire lawn, nearly spilling out into the street beyond. He owned this crowd, this town, this state. The pollsters and pundits had never understood his allure. The voters, the people, always had. They admired his strength. Nothing else mattered.

To the friendly crowd, he fired off a speech filled with sound bite after sound bite. "We must take back our streets."

The crowd roared. Adrenaline coursed through his veins as the back of his shirt grew moist. "We must rebuild our great cities."

The crowd roared louder and longer than before, lapping up Milbank's rhetoric like a pack of hungry dogs.

He waved his hands as if to try to silence the throng, but he didn't want silence. He wanted the roars to continue. He wanted them to keep shouting his name.

After allowing the noise to settle, he focused his attention beyond the crowd and stared right at the row of cameras at the rear. He sucked in a deep breath and then fired his final salvo. "Connecticut is on a path to greatness, to destiny. Nobody will stop our progress. *Nobody.*"

The crowd erupted.

The final line had been largely meaningless, a vague puffery generated by a speechwriter's pen. But as expected, the crowd wasn't nearly so discerning. He had whipped them into a frenzy, their whooping and howling now nearly deafening as he raised his hands in triumph. The image would make for great news and even better television. In what could have been one of his life's darkest nights, Milbank had shined.

"Thank you," he said over the sustained applause. "God bless all of you and our great state."

He stepped away from the microphone and headed offstage. His throat burned, and his shirt was drenched in sweat. But he had triumphed. The noise from the crowd lingered far longer than necessary as he slowly made his way out of view, waving and pointing at friendly faces before slipping into the back of his waiting car.

Terri slid in beside him. "A home run, sir." She handed him his water. "That couldn't have gone better."

As always, she was spot on. He had shown them what he needed to, displayed the qualities that Connecticut residents desperately wanted in their governor. More importantly, he had shown himself to possess the type of strength and resolve the voters would want in their next US senator.

Senator Long had officially announced his retirement after four terms, his twenty-four years in Washington coming to an end. Energized by the rabid crowd, Milbank was already looking well past November, well past a mere governor's race.

He didn't care about divorce or scandal. He was as popular as ever. He was untouchable, unstoppable. And he wanted Long's seat. *Now.*

His Senate race had just begun.

Chapter 57

Jack stood in an aisle near the middle of the Baby World store in Stamford. After a long day at work, he was multitasking during the evening—shopping, tracking news updates from the governor's speech at Greenwich Town Hall, and engaging in a furious text exchange with his wife. The last of these pursuits was not going particularly well.

"We don't need it," she had replied more than once as Jack sent her photo after photo of possible purchases. As a general matter, Amanda was right. Her older sister, Elizabeth, had given them more hand-me-down baby gear than they could possibly ever use, much of it still usable after Nate had taken his turn. For the most part, Jack was thrilled to see each reply, Amanda's assertions of *we don't need it* leading him to cross one item, and the resulting cost, off his imaginary list of things they needed to secure before his daughter's arrival.

But he felt differently about this dress. He held the hanger at arm's length and dangled the shiny pink fabric in front of him.

Somewhere in the most primal recesses of his brain originated a need to buy his unborn daughter a sparkly pink dress. The urge made no logical sense. To the extent this baby needed anything, it was not a dress, and certainly not one that looked suitable for a princess. And yet for reasons he could not possibly explain, this father needed to buy this dress.

He texted Amanda a picture.

Amanda: *We don't need it. She's not even born yet, and you want to buy her a party dress?*

Jack had started to type his response when a new message appeared.

Amanda: *It's really cute though.*

Aha! Jack: *I know. I really think I need to buy it.*

Amanda: *Well, you do have an eye for fashion.* She added a smiley emoji.

Her sarcastic point was well taken. Jack couldn't remember the last time he'd bought *himself* any new clothes to refresh his dated wardrobe. Every year at Christmas, Amanda made a few attempts to draw him out of his stock palette of blues and grays. That collection of fashionable gifts was neatly piled on the shelves of Jack's closet while he wore the same outmoded garb.

He held the tiny dress up one more time, thinking about the daughter he hoped one day would wear it. *What would she be like?*

A pregnant woman pushed a shopping cart past him. "Oh, that's adorable," she crooned, the evidence in favor of purchase now piling up. "You have to get that!"

He grinned. "I think so too."

Decision made. He placed the dress in his cart, gently laying it on top of the giant box of Nate's training pants.

Jack: *I'm buying it for her.*

Amanda: *I'm glad. It's adorable. She'll love it.*

Chapter 58

Kyle leaned across the passenger seat and opened the door for Bill Clayton. The grizzled seventy-year-old hopped in, the smell of cigar smoke wafting in with him.

In the circles of Connecticut journalism, Clayton was nothing short of a legend. He had once run the news desk at the *Hartford Courant*. His involuntary retirement from that paper had come soon after the publisher tried, and failed, to scuttle one of Clayton's features on a corrupt but extremely popular state senator. Clayton got a Pulitzer for his efforts, while the *Courant* got a black mark on its record for journalistic integrity.

Clayton's retirement didn't last long. Within months, he had raised the funds to launch the *Connecticut Record*, a weekly newspaper combining stories of local interest with traditional, hard-hitting journalism. While nobody would confuse Clayton's paper with the *Washington Post* or *New York Times*, it was attracting readers and making money. The backers were happy, and Clayton was in the business he loved.

Kyle, who'd known Clayton for years, had played no small part in the *Record*'s early success. From time to time, he had generously provided Clayton with critical insights into major criminal investigations and access to some key figures in the Capitol. The reporter understood that there was no free lunch and no free news. But Kyle's prices had typically been rather low, such as a bit of information that Clayton had unearthed or some generous coverage, including flattering photographs, of something that Kyle or the governor wanted the voters to see. Most recently, Clayton had dispatched one of his photographers to record the governor awarding Kyle a citation for bravery and generously allocated a quarter page of space to the resulting photo. Framed copies supplied by the paper now sat on Kyle's desk at work and his dresser at home. Kyle understood it had been a bald appeal to his vanity. It had worked.

"So, what do you have for me?" Clayton asked with a pencil in one hand and a pad in the other. Old school through and through.

"You know that lawyer who killed himself a couple weeks ago? Tom Nelson."

"The one from Greenwich? Found dead in his house, right?"

"Yup, that's him. Turns out he had quite the gambling problem."

Clayton jotted down the name. "Interesting."

"And the tox screen showed fentanyl. He was buying benzos on the street. Got a bad batch."

"I'm hearing a lot of stories like that." Clayton shook his head. "A real scourge."

"I know," Kyle said. "An ugly scene. And there's more. He had also stolen from an estate. The estate of Samuel Heller."

"Heller? With an H?"

"Yeah. Greenwich guy. Lived in a fancy house in backcountry. Died of cancer. Apparently, Nelson lifted the dead guy's watch, a family heirloom. The cops found it on him."

Clayton scribbled furiously. "Was he with a firm?"

"Collins, Warren, and Oswald." Kyle spelled out all three names.

"You working the case?"

"Nah, it's really a local matter. But I thought you'd be interested."

Clayton smiled. "Got it. Anything else?" The veteran reporter was savvy enough to smell a planted story. But he'd run it just the same.

"Nope, that's it for now. I guess you can just keep an ear out. That's all. Let me know if you happen to hear anything else about this estate or the law firm. I'll keep looking for your next great story."

"Sounds like a deal. Anything on the record?"

"Unnamed police source."

"Got it." Clayton finished writing and closed his notebook. He shook Kyle's hand. "A pleasure, as always."

"The pleasure is mine."

After the reporter left the car, Kyle breathed a sigh of relief. In retrospect, he had been foolish to swipe that watch. The theft was impulsive, unnecessary. He wasn't exactly thinking straight that morning. If he had been, he never would have pushed all the morphine into the ailing man's veins, "moving things along," as the governor had requested. But he would never admit those shortcomings to the others. And anyway, he'd now fixed it. The watch had been found on the dead lawyer's wrist, a *guilty* lawyer felled by a bad batch of drugs. The *Record* would tell that version of the story. That would make it the truth. That would end the matter.

Kyle had fixed it all. Once again.

Chapter 59

Jack stood as Jessica Baldwin entered the room and took her seat at the table.

"I've been seeing quite a bit of you," she observed as she fiddled with a set of papers on the tabletop.

"Yes, Your Honor," Jack replied as he retook his chair. In the weeks since Tom's death, he had been in court far more frequently than ever before, filing a string of petitions as he tried to wrap up some of the files Tom had left behind.

The matter before the court on this day was a relatively perfunctory closing of a small charitable trust of which Tom had been the trustee, a matter so uncontroversial that the Attorney General's office hadn't even bothered to send someone to attend the hearing. But as was her style, Judge Baldwin had insisted that Jack appear in person.

After the matter at hand was summarily resolved, she offered him a cup of coffee and an earful of conversation.

She was full of questions. *How was Jack managing in the aftermath of Tom's death? Had Jack spoken to Tom's daughter lately? Had Jack given thoughts to a replacement?* Her interest seemed genuine, her concern heartfelt.

Jack knew better. He had no desire to engage in this banter, but he couldn't afford to let the opportunity pass. If he kept her engaged, a clue might slip off her tongue.

Five minutes later, Jack was ready to abandon that effort. She was full of questions but offered neither answers nor information. If anyone was fishing, it was her. It was time to go.

Jack looked at his phone. "I'm sorry, Your Honor, I have a meeting back at the office."

She stood from the table, which signaled he was free to do the same. He shook her hand.

"Thank you, Your Honor. It was a pleasure to be in your court."

"The pleasure was mine." She smiled. "Oh, by the way, did I hear you're expecting?"

Jack's breath caught. "Um, yes," he said. "A little while longer," he added, consciously not being more specific about the baby.

"Oh, that's wonderful. Little girls are so much fun! You must be so excited."

A chill ran down his spine. *Did he hear her right?*

"We have a son, Nate."

"And a little sister on the way. He must be so excited."

There was no confusing it. How the hell did she know?

"Yes, it's an exciting time." Realizing his fists were clenched, he forced his hands to relax.

"I'm sure. I think it's wonderful," she said, seemingly unaware of the panic she'd just induced.

Chapter 60

Daniel Milbank smiled as his pollsters left his office. Their weekly briefing could not have been more upbeat. The massive environmental bill had generated both the publicity he had hoped for and an infusion of campaign donations, many of them from the major national companies that would now increasingly dominate the retail gasoline market. What had once been a two-point deficit had grown to a solid seven-point lead.

Even the cities were turning his way. His investments in Waterbury and New Haven were paying off as funds slipped into the pockets of community leaders led to droves of newly registered voters prepared to cast their ballots for him. In Bridgeport, dear old Marcus Price had delivered on his promise of support since the Milbank campaign had generously contributed to the restoration of his beloved community center after that tragic, still-unexplained fire nearly burned it to the ground.

The trends were all good. Milbank could taste victory, a major one. His almost-assured reelection was just one part of what looked to be a far more sweeping achievement. His party appeared likely to retain control of the General Assembly and to take control of the Senate. And thus, with his power consolidated, he could increasingly reward his friends, punish his enemies, and line his own pockets in the process.

He kicked his feet up on the desk and thought about that future. The days of petty theft from Greenwich estates would yield to a far more comprehensive system of self-enrichment. It was his moment, time for the scrappy kid from the city to solidify his position among the elite. He almost salivated as he thought about it.

From there, it would be ever upward, this reelection campaign blending into one for the US Senate. The path was laid out before him with nothing to stand in his way.

A knock on the door roused him from his daydream. He straightened his chair and dropped his feet back onto the floor. "Come in."

Brian Lockwood strode in, a pair of staffers trailing a few steps behind him. "Good afternoon, Governor," Lockwood said in the formal tone he used when other members of the staff were around. "Can we talk about the Boston trip?"

In an attempt to develop more national exposure, the governor had become a frequent traveler, setting off to destinations near and far to bolster his name recognition and political credentials. The trips had taken him as far away as Europe and the Middle East, taxpayer-funded junkets that likely did more for Milbank's political aspirations than they helped the people of Connecticut. Next week would take him only as far as Boston, where he was scheduled to give the keynote address at a major tax conference. He wasn't exactly an expert in the nuances of tax policy, but he saw nothing wrong with spending a couple nights in Boston on the taxpayers' dime.

"Of course. I'd almost forgotten about that," Milbank said. "The tax lawyer thing, right? What's the plan?"

"Yes, sir. You're speaking on Thursday." Lockwood glanced down at his tablet. "We have you going up early Wednesday, lunch with Governor Lee in your hotel suite, a few donor meetings, and then a small dinner at the Harvard Club."

"How many are we expecting at dinner?"

"Eighty-five or so. Maybe ninety."

Milbank did the math. That would net over a quarter million in campaign donations, assuming they were charging the going rate.

"Then the speech Thursday," Lockwood continued. "Leave immediately after. Back home by dinnertime."

"Can we stop on the way home? How about a photo op at UConn and then dinner at that place in town, the little diner?"

"The Springs?"

"Yeah, that one. Nice guy who owns that place," Milbank said, thinking about the owner's wife and how her blouse had gaped open the last time he'd seen her. "Let's make sure I get a photo with him and his wife."

"I'll set it up."

"And we're good at the Van Buren, right?"

"Yes, sir. You're booked in the Presidential Suite."

"You're so good to me."

Lockwood beamed. "Thank you, sir." His eyes then drifted toward the floor. "Um... the only issue is the detail." He paused. "Sharon thinks you should have at least three with you."

Milbank groaned. "I really don't want to spend two hours in a car full of troopers."

"Then take two cars," Lockwood replied without hesitation. "Kyle can drive yours. Let the other two trail."

The governor rubbed his temples. As much as he disliked the thought of extra eyes following his movements, a larger security detail would make a statement, one he wouldn't mind being captured by the photographers in Boston: *This is an important man. A powerful one.*

"That's fine," he said. "Two cars."

"Great. We'll set it up. Anything else, sir?"

"I think we're good, Brian. Thanks for everything."

Chapter 61

Jack sat at his desk, his cell phone in front of him. His gut seized as the first text message came in.

Joe: *Bad news, bud.*

Jack steeled himself and typed out his reply: *What's going on?*

Joe: *Dead ends. Higher-ups here looked at it all. Everyone agrees it was an accidental death. No interest in exploring anything else. So it's done.*

Jack: *No surprise. We drop it?*

Joe: *I think so. There's nothing here.*

Jack: *Got it. Time to move on and get back to practicing law.*

Joe: *Yup. Just try to put this all behind you.*

Jack: *I will.*

Joe: *I'm sorry again about your partner.*

Jack: *Thanks for everything. Let's catch up when you have more time.*

Joe: *Yes. On vacation next week but then let's catch up after?*

Jack: *Good idea. Thanks again.*

Joe: *You're welcome. Sorry I couldn't be more help.*

Jack slid that phone aside then turned his attention to the second cell phone, a shiny new one, sitting on his desk. He popped in a set of earphones. "How was that?" he asked.

"Perfect," Joe Andrews replied. "Absolutely perfect."

"You think it will work?"

"Time will tell. Remember to keep using that phone a bit. Chatty stuff. Nothing too private. Nothing important."

"Got it. So, I guess I'll see you on Wednesday, then?"

"Yes, sir. Looking forward to it. Chinese sound good? Chicken and broccoli still your go to?"

"Yeah, but I don't expect I'll have much of an appetite."

"Come on, bud. You'll be fine. I've dealt with way tougher characters than this lot, and so have you."

"I hope you're right."

"I'm always right. I'll see you on Wednesday."

Chapter 62

Kyle opened his eyes as the final notes of *Taps* reverberated off the rows of rain-slicked headstones. He held his right arm tight against his body, a folded flag pressed between his elbow and ribs. A muddy pile of dirt surrounded the hole in which his father's casket had been lowered just moments earlier. Assuming this morning counted as visiting his father, it was the first time in several years he had done so.

As the bugler fell silent, the military chaplain closed his bible and placed his hand on Kyle's shoulder. "He was proud of you. He said you were a man of integrity."

Kyle's eyes moistened. *Integrity, huh.* His father wasn't exactly the authority on that. "Thank you, Padre," Kyle replied, suppressing the urge to say what he really felt. He shook the man's hand before turning away. *He'd had enough of this.*

"He spoke of you often in his final days," the chaplain said.

Out of courtesy more than curiosity, Kyle turned back to face him.

The chaplain nodded. "He told me of your troubles as well."

Kyle's jaw dropped. "Excuse me?"

"He said I should tell you that he understands what you did. He wanted you to know he was proud."

Kyle didn't give a crap about the chaplain's false praise. The man sounded like he was reading the words from a greeting card. Kyle did, however, wonder just what the hell the chaplain was talking about. "I'm sorry, but I'm not following you. My father was an addict. You know that, right?"

"I do. He was, and that demon plagued him right to the end. But that didn't change how he felt about you. Not one bit."

Whatever. This is a funeral, not a therapy session. Way too late for that. "Okay, thanks again." He began to turn away again.

"And he never forgot what you did for that girl."

Kyle froze. *What the hell?* For the first time in years, he felt compelled to try to understand his father. And this might be his final chance. "I'm really not following this. What girl are you talking about?"

"The one you got arrested for. The one with drugs in your car."

Kyle could taste the egg sandwich he'd wolfed down on his way there. "I don't know what my old man tried to tell you, but the only drugs in any car belonged to my father. And yeah, I took the fall for him. Maybe I shouldn't have. He didn't deserve it. But there was no girl involved. I really have no clue what you're talking about."

The chaplain frowned. "Perhaps we're not thinking about the same story."

"Okay." Kyle sighed. "Then what story are you talking about?"

"Your father told me that years ago, you were arrested when drugs were found in your car. You were a man of honor, never telling the police they weren't yours. Instead, you took the fall, refusing to clear your own name by implicating someone else."

"Yeah, that's the story. Yet another time my old man screwed me."

The chaplain cocked his head. "But that's where our stories seem to go different ways." His tone held a hint of uncertainty.

"I'm the one who knows what happened," Kyle said assuredly. "Those were my old man's drugs. More poison he had brought into his life... and mine. Another parole violation. Another stumble that could have sent him back. And how does he respond? He disappears and leaves me behind to take the fall for him. Yet again. End of story." His hands were clenched into fists at his sides. *Enough.* He spun and walked away.

"Those weren't your father's drugs," the chaplain called after him.

"Yeah, right," Kyle scoffed without turning around.

"He'd loaned his car to the girl," the chaplain boomed, all uncertainty now gone from his tone. "The judge's daughter. They were hers."

A bolt of pain shot across Kyle's forehead. He stopped and turned around. "*What?*"

"The drugs were your friend's. You were protecting her, correct?" The chaplain nodded as he headed toward Kyle.

"Protecting *her?*" Kyle squinted, the pain now searing from ear to ear.

"Jessica!" the chaplain exclaimed as if proud to have remembered the detail. "He said her name was Jessica."

"My father said they were Jessica's drugs?"

The chaplain nodded. "Yes." His eyebrows drew together. "But you knew that, right?"

Every muscle in Kyle's body tensed, and his pulse suddenly beat with fury as waves of pain lapped across his temples. The chaplain tried to place a soothing hand on Kyle's shoulder, but Kyle dodged the man's touch.

The chaplain dropped his hand. "Your father may have been too caught up in his own problems to adequately help you with yours," the chaplain said. "But as to those drugs, he was as innocent as you."

Chapter 63

The Cos Cob section of Greenwich once had been a working-class neighborhood with modest houses set on equally modest lots. The changing landscape and inflated real estate prices no longer seemed to reflect that history. Two- and three-bedroom capes and colonials had been systematically expanded and renovated, resulting in four- and five-bedroom McMansions featuring designer kitchens, luxury baths, and the price tags to go with them. But a small red colonial on Jackson Street seemed to have been left behind by the progress. Built in 1939, the home had remained in the same family ever since.

Jack followed Amanda through the front door and immediately knew that this house was unlike all the others they had seen on this Saturday morning. The hardwood floors were dinged and imperfect. The kitchen was neat but outdated, the simple white cabinets a good twenty years old. The living room was large enough for family gatherings but not for lavish parties. The place looked like a home instead of a showcase.

The agent slapped her palm on the plaster separating the living room from the kitchen. "You could probably knock this wall down and really open up this space. You'd need a structural engineer to be sure"—she tapped on the wall—"but I would bet you can support the span with steel. Open floorplans are all the rage."

Jack thought about how much simpler life must have been back in 1939, when a wall was considered a useful thing for holding up a house rather than an impediment to an open floorplan.

They walked up a set of creaky stairs. As they made their way down the hall of the second floor, Jack peeked through each doorway.

"Functional," the agent muttered as she paused outside the first bathroom so they could get a better look.

The bathroom was simple in layout and design. It had been updated a decade or so ago with clean white fixtures—no gleaming brass, no honed marble—but was still constrained within its original footprint.

The agent led them through the two other bedrooms, both of modest size, and showed them the other bathroom, which mirrored the first.

This was not the type of home Jack had dreamed he might someday be able to afford. But it was the home he had always pictured himself living in. "What do you think?" he asked his wife as they entered the master bedroom, a front-facing room only slightly larger than the other two.

"It's cute," she replied. *Not exactly a rave.*

"Cute as in 'way too small'?"

"No." She looked up at the ceiling.

He followed her gaze and noticed the heft of the original crown moldings, the subtle swirls of vintage plaster. Nothing built today could replicate that look.

"Actually, cute as in *charming*," she said. "It's cozy."

The agent beckoned them back into the hallway. "Let's take a look at the yard."

She led them downstairs and then into the backyard. A small slate patio lay next to a grassy area just large enough to toss a football. The cedar fence that surrounded the yard on three sides looked old but sturdy. Jack pictured Nate running around in this space, joined, in time, by his little sister. He walked onto the lawn and eyed the weeds growing amid the grass.

"You can have all of that treated," the agent said. "Probably cut back some of those old trees to get more light in here. It would help open this up a bit. Of course, you could always rip this all out and go with new sod."

He scanned across the yard and imagined Nate picking the dandelions scattered about the imperfect lawn. He looked back at Amanda. She was cradling her stomach with one hand, gently rubbing it with the other. Her eyes were closed, her head tilted up toward the warm sun.

Chapter 64

Kyle sat at his kitchen table and stared at the flickering screen of his laptop. He tallied the numbers on the spreadsheet again. Just over seven million remained in his various offshore accounts. Plus, he still had the balance from that final million he had extracted from the Heller estate.

The other two knew nothing of the details set out in these spreadsheets. They had wanted their hands clean, the paper trail pointing right to Kyle and ending long before their lofty doorsteps. They had trusted him to play his assigned role of blindly repaying his old debt to the kindhearted Baldwins and loyally serving the governor who had given him a chance nobody else would. They must have thought him such a fool. But now he knew better. Now he finally knew the truth.

The truth was he had never owed Jessica anything. Far from it. Her teenage lie had defined the course of Kyle's entire adult life. She had destroyed his father's legacy and nearly cost Kyle his freedom and his future. *She* was the one who had long owed *him* everything. It was time for her to settle her tab.

He didn't know for sure how many people besides Jessica had been playing him for the fool. He wondered if Jessica's father had really been the merciful figure Kyle remembered or if he had he simply been saving his daughter's hide while willingly using Kyle as the sacrificial lamb. The answers had likely died with the old man.

And what about Milbank? Was he in on the decades-long deception? Did he know the real reason why Kyle needed a little help to clear his background check? Or was he, too, a victim of Jessica's duplicity, believing Kyle's true story to be the one she had written for him? In the end, none of that really mattered. Even if nobody else knew it, the reality was that Kyle had spent decades repaying a debt he'd never owed. The millions he'd squirreled offshore had once seemed like a fair price to level the score, to repay the old debt. In fact, he had gotten a raw deal.

All that was about to change.

With thundering keystrokes, he initiated a series of wire transfers, moving nearly eight million dollars from account to account, nation to nation. The paper trail Kyle was setting into place would be impossible to unwind. The money would be gone. *All* of it. *Every last cent.*

And soon, so would he. Off to Granby, at least for a while. And then perhaps even further off the grid. He would slip over a border to someplace law enforcement couldn't reach. He knew the list by heart. The Maldives, Bosnia, Morocco. All countries that thumbed their noses at US law enforcement. All places he could start anew and live in opulence without fear of extradition, the prior sad chapters of his life abandoned half a world away.

Kyle closed the laptop and cracked open a celebratory beer. He nearly drained it in one extended guzzle. This was not the end he had envisioned, not the way he had always thought this chapter of his life would come to a close. But the more he thought about it, the more he realized he would have his happy ending.

He went into the bedroom to pack a bag for his upcoming trip to Boston. He needed to take one last journey with the governor, one final time together before Kyle simply disappeared.

Chapter 65

"Hey, anyone ever audit your books, Agent Andrews?" Jack teased as he took in the impressive view from Joe Andrews's Boston apartment. Jack was captivated by the subtle shifts of light and color as the city slowly transformed from day to night. "Not sure how you afford this place on a government salary."

"Family money," Joe replied, his tone sounding like he was joking, even though both men knew he was not. "Dr. and Dr. Andrews have taken good care of me."

Jack laughed and took a sip of beer as he turned away from the window.

Joe hoisted a brown bag in the air. "And dinner is on me." He tore open the sack and began piling cartons of Chinese food on the table.

Jack stared at the ridiculous amount of food. "You buy out the store?"

"Kinda. It's twenty percent off on Wednesdays."

"There better be some chicken and broccoli somewhere in there."

Joe raised a carton above his head. "Here you are, Your Majesty. The finest chicken and broccoli in all the land." He handed Jack the container. "Hey, I thought you said you wouldn't be hungry?"

Jack popped open the carton. "I'm not really, but free chicken and broccoli is not something I can simply ignore." He grabbed a plate and plopped some white rice on it before adding the chicken and broccoli.

Joe filled his plate with some lo mein noodles and a healthy portion of shrimp. "So, let's put it all together."

"Okay," Jack said. "We know Kyle is dirty. Judge Baldwin is probably involved. And they may not be working alone. Oh, and we really don't have any proof of anything, except for the very clear trail that points to my dead partner."

"Excellent summary!" Joe grabbed his glass and raised it. "A toast to all our conjecture."

"And absolutely no proof." Jack clinked his bottle against Joe's glass.

"And by the way," Joe said in a more serious tone, "I never underestimate the amount of corruption in the world. I'm willing to bet Baldwin isn't the top of the food chain."

"How high could it go?" Jack stuffed a sprig of broccoli in his mouth.

"Who knows? But maybe tonight is the night we find out. Jenny Levine's the best I got," he said, referring to the agent that had been assigned to trail Kyle while in Boston. "Maybe my agent outsmarts your trooper?"

"Wouldn't that be awesome?"

Joe nodded. "It would. And I hope it happens. But I have to tell you, if we come up empty…"

Jack paused with a piece of chicken on his fork. "What?"

Joe sighed. "Look. I don't want to blow smoke at you, so here's the deal. My version of the summary is even more damning than yours. Right now, we've got a dead lawyer with a gambling problem who overdosed on street drugs wearing a stolen watch. Oh, and a paper trail of stolen money points straight to him."

"I know, but—"

Joe raised his hand and pointed a half-eaten eggroll at Jack "Hear me out. The dead guy's law partner insists a demented woman is sure a state trooper named Kyle is really the mastermind, but she also thinks this Kyle is a general. Oh yeah, and this general, or trooper, whatever he is, grew up in the same town as a judge, so she must be in on it because there's never a coincidence in life. So there you have it, folks. Case closed." He clapped his hands together as if cleaning the proverbial dust from them. "I have that about right?"

Jack set his plate back on the table, his fleeting appetite having disappeared. "Well, if you want to look at it that way..."

"It *is* that way, Jack. And the truth is, there's no way I can convince my counterparts in New Haven to investigate a state trooper and a sitting judge on those facts. I promise you, I've tried. It's not going to happen."

"What exactly are you saying?"

"I'm saying it's you and me, bud. Just like old times. And I'm also saying this. I've gone about as far as I can go. If we don't get something more solid soon, we're going to need to just walk away."

Chapter 66

Kyle stepped into the lobby of the Van Buren Hotel a pace ahead of Daniel Milbank. Their return on this evening was bit more low-key than their exit had been just a few hours earlier, the pair of uniformed troopers who had escorted the governor during the day having been discharged for the night. They were now just two men in nondescript suits, the governor and his right-hand man walking through a deserted hotel lobby.

"Good evening, Governor Milbank," the man at the front desk said, snapping to obsequious attention. "Is there anything I can do for you, sir?" He kept his adoring eyes locked on the governor, while Kyle's very existence seemed to have gone unnoticed.

"I'm fine, thank you." Milbank nodded at the man. "Thank you for all your hard work. I really appreciate it," he added, offering one of his usual platitudes.

Kyle turned to the elevators. *And thanks from me too. You've done so much to make my stay more pleasant.*

After a quick elevator ride to the penthouse, they arrived at the governor's suite. Once inside, Kyle performed a quick sweep of the rooms, an act required by protocol but rather unnecessary in reality. There would be no listening devices planted by a foreign government, no assassin hiding behind the ornate curtains. Milbank frankly wasn't that important, at least outside of his own mind. The latest polling data showed that only three percent of Americans outside of New England could even recall his name, a number unlikely to attract the attention of the Russians or Chinese.

"We're good, sir," Kyle reported.

"Great. What time is she getting here?"

"Twenty-five minutes or so. I'll meet her at the loading dock."

Milbank checked his watch. "I'm going to clean up a bit. You mind hanging out until she gets closer?"

"Not at all." Kyle sat in a chair. He pulled out his phone and scrolled through his texts.

Fifteen minutes later, the freshly showered governor emerged from the bathroom, wrapped in a fluffy white bathrobe. His hair was neatly combed. His five-o'clock shadow was gone, and an aroma of cologne now wafted behind him.

"Do you mind if I use your sink?" Kyle asked.

"Um, sure," Milbank replied.

"Thanks. I think they need to clean their windowsills," Kyle pointed toward the curtains. "I touched something a bit sticky over there."

While Milbank continued to the bedroom, Kyle stepped onto the marble floor of the bathroom and closed the door behind him. He marveled at the ornate fixtures made of gleaming porcelain with solid brass knobs. His room five floors below bore no resemblance to the opulence of the penthouse.

He stood in front of the wood-and-marble vanity inset with two sinks. The governor's toiletries were laid out neatly beside the sink on the left, so Kyle shifted toward the right. He pulled a tube of lipstick from his pocket and nestled it into a corner of the pink granite countertop.

He chuckled as he thought of the name of the color marked on the lipstick's cap. Adulterous red. The irony was rich.

He adjusted the tube one final time then returned to his chair in the living room. Soon, the governor entered, fully dressed and holding his bathrobe in his hand.

Kyle sprang from his seat. "I'll hang that up for you," he said in hopes of keeping the governor from returning to the bathroom.

"Thanks." Milbank handed off the robe. "Are you going downstairs to wait for her?"

Kyle took the garment. "Yes, sir," he said as he crossed the room. "She should be here in just a few minutes. I've got the freight elevator blocked off. We'll come straight up." He hung the robe on a hook beside the door.

Milbank nodded. "Good."

"Will you need anything else after that?"

"Nope. Bring her up and we should be good. I'll text you in the morning. No later than six."

"Very good, sir. I'll be waiting."

Chapter 67

Jack stepped out of the lobby of Joe's building and into the Boston evening. The bright lights and busy sidewalks reminded him of his time in New York City. As a throng of pedestrians streamed around him, his thoughts drifted back to the past, to that office on the forty-fourth floor, the power and prestige that had been everywhere around him, the heady sensation that came from making the big money, from working at the big firm. He missed only a few things about those days, the most prominent of which was the nonstop rush of adrenaline, the unending exhilaration.

But there had been downsides to that world, plenty of them. He'd learned that lesson just in time, but perhaps not perfectly. At CWO, he'd drifted into the same danger, sliding backward toward the same mistakes he had made years earlier. He'd worried too much about others' definitions of success, trying to grow his law firm into something that was the envy of all. He'd thought about buying places he could never afford, houses designed to impress rather than shelter. He now knew better than that. He needed a career. He needed a home. He needed his family. He needed nothing else.

By that metric, he had everything: a great job, loyal friends and partners, an adoring wife, one child to cherish, and another on the way. Two generations of Collins lawyers before him had defined their success without any reference to a balance sheet. There had been no fancy houses, no fancy cars. But there had been plenty of joy.

He tapped his watch and called home.

"Hi, sweetheart," Amanda whispered.

"Nate asleep?"

"Just went down. So far so good."

He turned the corner onto a slightly less populated street. "And how are you holding up?"

"Me? I'm fine. Not bad."

"That's not exactly a rave."

"You try having your stomach pushed up into your lungs and see how you feel."

"Understood." He came to a crosswalk and scanned for traffic before proceeding. "I miss you."

"I miss you too." The smile came through in her tone.

"I'll be home tomorrow night. The train gets in about ten."

"Will you forgive me if I don't wait up?"

"Of course. You need your rest." He stopped at the next corner. "Hey, I've been thinking more about those houses."

"Me too," she replied.

"And?" He steeled himself in anticipation of her response.

"I really love that one on Jackson Street."

"Me too." A sense of calm overtook him as he crossed another street and neared his hotel. "There's no ocean view though."

"That's okay. Who wants to look out the window when I've got you to look at?"

His eyes moistened. "Did you practice that line?"

"Several times."

"I like it. And I *love* you."

"I love you too. Wake me up when you get home. Oh, and good luck on your speech."

"Thanks." He'd nearly forgotten about that. "I'll see you tomorrow."

"Have a good night. And get home safe."

"I will."

Chapter 68

Kyle peered down the length of the bar, checking out the crowd, which predominantly consisted of college students. Technically, as the head of Milbank's travel security detail, Kyle was on duty. But the governor was safely tucked into his suite at the Van Buren with Jessica Baldwin. They had politely told Kyle to beat it for the rest of the night and let them violate their marital vows in peace. That left Kyle free to spend the night in this run-down bar near Fenway Park, a baseball cap pulled down low on his head and a pint of beer sitting in front of him. It was not a bad gig.

Kyle would receive a text message at some point before six in the morning. At that time, his assignment would be the same as it was on all of these trips. He would need to get to the governor's suite before Milbank's handlers arrived and make sure everything was ready for the new day. First and foremost, that would mean ensuring that Milbank was alone with no trace of whatever woman may have spent all or part of the night in the governor's room. Tonight, as was often but not exclusively the case, the guest of honor was Jessica Baldwin. So tomorrow, Kyle would help evict her and ensure that no evidence of her visit was left behind. Until then, the night was his.

He looked at his empty glass then checked the time on his phone. He glanced around at the bar's young clientele and wondered if he should just turn in for the night. He waved at the bartender, though he hadn't decided if he wanted another drink or to pay his tab.

Someone flopped onto the barstool beside him. "Yankees suck," the interloper said before cackling. The kid wore a Boston College sweatshirt and a Red Sox cap.

Kyle turned back toward the bartender and signaled again.

The kid tapped him on the shoulder. "Did you hear me?" His breath reeked of cheap beer. "Take the cap off. You're in Red Sox country."

"Just calm down, buddy. Ease back, okay?" Kyle looked at the two others standing behind their drunk companion. "Why don't you guys take him out of here and get him some coffee?"

"Why don't you just piss off?" the kid on the barstool said.

Kyle took a slow breath in and counted to three. *Defuse the situation. The kid's just drunk. Pay the bill and walk away. Just walk away.*

He stood and took a step away from the drunk. He waved to the bartender one more time, putting his whole arm into it.

The bartender finally responded. "Give me a sec, hon. I'll be right there."

Kyle started to sit down again, his back to the drunk kid. He felt a tug on his hair, and his baseball cap went flying. The annoying cackle rang out again. Kyle spun around, ready for whatever the young man wanted to dish out.

The drunk grinned sloppily. "That's better."

Kyle grabbed the kid by the wrist and spun him around to face the bar. He pulled his shield from his pocket and shoved it in the drunk's face then raised it in the air. "Police officer!" he yelled as he pressed his knee into the small of the jerk's back, ignoring the kid's wailing.

Kyle jerked the guy back around and stared into his glazed, panicked eyes. "You need to grow up." He shoved the kid toward his two buddies. "All of you, get the hell out of here."

The two sidekicks manage to catch their friend before he fell on his face. All three bolted for the door.

A woman behind him laughed. When Kyle turned around, a tall brunette held out his Yankees cap.

"I think this belongs to you," she said. "Are you really a cop?"

He accepted his hat and put it back on his head. "Yeah. Connecticut state police."

"Connecticut's that way," she said, pointing past the bar.

"I know. I'm on a travel detail."

"Well, I'm glad you stopped by then. You know, that guy spent the last ten minutes staring at my chest. Thanks for getting rid of him."

"My pleasure," he said. "I should probably settle up and get going."

"There's nothing to settle up. You drink on me tonight."

He shook his head. "That's not necessary."

"It's the least I can do. But the deal is only good if you'll hang out a little longer."

"I really need to go. I've got an early morning."

"Come on." She placed her fingertips on his arm. "I work for a mutual fund company. You just gave me more excitement than I get in a week of work. I can't imagine what the rest of the night could bring."

Chapter 69

Kyle mentally counted how many policies and procedures he had violated in the last few hours. He decided that beating on the Red Sox fan didn't count. He could chalk that one up to self-defense. But since the brunette had stepped into his night, the number had gone way up. He'd had too much to drink while on duty, probably gotten a little too detailed in the war stories of some of his most high-profile matters, and definitely been way too transparent in his attempts to get her back to his hotel room. That was three. There were probably more.

She'd brought out the worst side of him. He also couldn't figure her out, not even a little. She'd thrown back shots as if they were filled with water. She'd deflected almost every question about herself. She'd removed his hand from her knee, more than once, with a grip that seemed awfully strong for that of a mutual fund manager.

If he didn't know better, he would have pegged her as FBI. But the FBI wasn't interested in him. He'd seen the texts to prove it. *So who exactly is she?*

She excused herself from the table and returned toting another round of beers.

Kyle groaned. "No way." His head was pounding.

"You have someplace better to be?" she asked, pouting.

"No, but I've got an early morning."

"So do I." She raised her glass.

"Fine." He hoisted his glass to match hers and looked into her brown eyes. The alcohol hadn't dulled Kyle's honed instincts. Something didn't feel right.

She took a long drink then leaned closer to him. "Let's say I wanted to make some money disappear?" she asked, her words sounding more slurred than they had before. "Maybe I'm in the middle of a nasty divorce, just to pick a random example." She smiled mischievously then bit her lip. "Hypothetically, of course, how would I screw over my cheating husband?"

Finally, it all made sense. She was a scorned wife prowling a Boston bar for revenge in one form or another.

Or maybe not?

He eyed her carefully, her face revealing no hint of her true emotions. That story was just a bit too convenient. And too late. A final Hail Mary attempt to play the damsel in distress— an appeal to his masculinity, and his vanity. It was straight out of a training manual. Maybe she was a cop after all. There was one sure way to find out.

He leaned over and whispered in her ear, "Let's go back to my room. We'll teach that husband of yours a lesson, and I'll tell you everything you want to know." It was a fair trade, one a wife looking for revenge would probably entertain but one a cop would never accept.

"It's so tempting." She shook her head. "But I can't. I'm still married."

The hair on the back of his neck rose.

It was time to get the hell out of there.

Chapter 70

Jessica Baldwin carried two steaming cups of coffee into the bedroom. She put one on each nightstand then slipped back into bed.

"What the hell time is it?" Daniel Milbank asked, rolling over to face her.

"Almost six o'clock."

He turned back over and swatted at the clock on his nightstand. "More like a quarter after five. Go back to sleep."

"I can't sleep. We need to talk."

"Come on, Jess. I have a big speech today. I need some sleep."

She sat up and fumbled around her nightstand for the light switch. She flipped it up, bathing the room in light. "We *need* to talk," she snapped.

"What the hell?" He propped himself up on his elbows, squinting against the brightness. "Talk about what?"

"Where is all this going?"

"You're not really asking me that now, are you? At five in the morning?"

"Five fifteen."

He flopped back down. "Seriously? I'm in the middle of a campaign. This thing with Cindy at the house is still fresh news. Your timing is terrible."

"Oh, spare me. You can think about me and a campaign at the same time. And don't you dare play the family-trauma game. You haven't given a crap about Cindy for years. You probably would have loved for that guy to finish her off."

He sat all the way up and stared down at her. "What the hell is wrong with you?" His face filled with crimson fury. "This isn't the time for this conversation. Period."

As he was prone to doing, the good governor had gotten incredibly angry incredibly quickly. Judging from her racing heart, she had joined him. She had sworn to herself that she wasn't going to do this now. Yet, she found herself unable to stop. She'd reached the unbearable final straw. Perhaps it was once again being snuck into a hotel room via a freight elevator, treated like the governor's cheap whore rather than his supposed true love. More likely, it was seeing a tube of red lipstick sitting on the marble countertop of his bathroom. A garish, bright, red. The color of lust, and of betrayal.

"Who is she?"

"What are you talking about?"

"Did you even catch her name?"

He scoffed, an arrogant, dismissive sound. "What the hell is that supposed to mean?"

She suddenly realized her plan to talk to him had gone way off the rails. She needed to get him back on track. "Danny, are we ever going to do this right? Or is this all we're ever going to be?"

He noticed the coffee on the nightstand, picked up the cup, and took a sip. "Thanks for the coffee." His tone had softened to match hers. "Jess, you know I love you, right?" He reached out and ran a finger down her cheek. "It's just not the right time. Once I'm in the Senate, things will all be different. I promise."

She crossed her arms over her chest. Another promise. He'd made plenty of those.

He patted her shoulder. "Just hang in there for a few more years."

A few more years.

He was right, of course. This was the wrong time, entirely wrong. He needed to win this election. He needed to lock down the Senate seat. There could be neither divorce nor public romance nor hint of scandal. He was entirely right.

She gazed into his eyes, and they betrayed him. He may love her, but he didn't mourn their tragic lot the way she did. He didn't crave their future together with the same zeal.

"Hey, listen," he said. "I've got a big speech to give in a couple of hours. So you should probably sneak back out of here before my entourage shows up. I'll text Kyle to come pick you up, okay?"

And there it was. She hated this part. A quick shower. Gathering her stuff. Sneaking out into the wee hours of the morning before the staff showed up, her time with the great governor spent as a vampire unable to see the bright light of day. The whole affair made her feel cheap and dirty. In fact, everything he had just said made her feel that way. They had their arrangement. She was to bide her time and play her part. This wasn't love. It never had been.

She went into the bathroom and closed the door. When she turned on the shower, she spun the dial to make the water as hot as she could stand it. As she stood under the steamy spray, she used a sudsy washcloth to scrub all traces of him from her body. She needed to cleanse herself of Daniel Milbank before she snuck back out into the Boston morning. She might have been the power behind the throne, but she had most assuredly never been the queen.

Chapter 71

Kyle gently placed his arm behind Jessica Baldwin's back as he escorted her out of the governor's suite. She wore no makeup. Her hair was still wet. Yet, unlike Kyle, she didn't look hungover.

"The car's waiting for you downstairs," he said as they walked down the hallway. "I'll take you down."

She jerked away from his hand. "Don't treat me like that."

"Like what?"

"Like I'm some whore you need to make sure leaves quietly."

"I wasn't thinking that at all," he lied. "We just need to be careful. We don't need anyone seeing you here."

"And did you take *her* out this way too?"

"Her?"

"Don't play dumb, Kyle. And you're losing your touch. She left her lipstick behind."

"I don't know what you're talking about." He dug his nails into his palm to help him suppress a smile. *Screw you. I owe you this pain and so much more.*

"Like hell you don't."

"Whatever you say, Jess." As much fun as this was, he was way too tired to deal with her right now. He needed to get her out of there and then get himself into a hot shower. "Let's just get you to the car."

"Drop the attitude." She quickened her pace and reached the elevator bank with him trailing a step behind. She pushed the down button.

"Not that one. Over here," he said, pointing at the next set of doors. Establishing his control, he gently took her elbow and guided her to the freight elevator. He pulled out a key and inserted it, then pushed the button for the basement.

As the cab descended, their tension failed to abate. The lipstick had been a subtle jab. Kyle decided it was time to throw a roundhouse. "You know, Jess, he's never leaving her. He's talked about it, but it's not happening. You should have heard him after the break-in. He was blathering like a fool, talking about how much Cindy meant to him."

She didn't immediately reply, but her face revealed her pain. Her eyes moistened. She sniffled, then bit a quivering lip. "Screw you," she finally muttered.

"I'm sorry, Jess. You deserve to know. You deserve the *truth*." He emphasized the last word for himself not her. *The truth. The painful truth.*

The freight elevator lurched to a stop. A nondescript hallway would lead them to the alley behind the hotel. Once there, he could dump her into the car and be done with her.

As the elevator doors opened, she lunged toward the buttons and jabbed the one for the lobby.

"What the hell are you doing?" Kyle asked. "The car's down here."

"Then have it brought around front. I'm leaving through the lobby."

"The car's waiting."

"Then have them move it! I'm done with the slinking around. I am walking out of the lobby of this hotel."

"Jess—"

"Don't *Jess* me. I'll scream bloody murder. You want *that*? Know your place. I go where I want."

Know my place? She'd played that card way too often, and far too long.

"Fine." He tapped out a text to the driver, telling him to move the car to the hotel's main entrance. He didn't care anymore anyway. If someone saw her here, she could have the scandal. She deserved it.

His mind raced as the elevator rose back toward the lobby. He pictured a scandal, an epic one. Ethical investigations. Paparazzi circling like buzzards. *Oh yeah, she deserves that.* It was a brilliant idea. The perfect ending.

When the doors slid open, they stepped out of the car and onto the polished marble floor. A single clerk stood behind the front desk. He offered a far too cheerful "Good morning" given the obscenely early hour.

Kyle fell a few feet behind as Jessica greeted the clerk. She strolled through the lobby, heading for the front door. Her shoulders were back. Her head was held high.

She had no idea what lay ahead.

Chapter 72

A hint of the coming sunrise brightened the sky as Jack walked down Congress Street. He had been thrilled to have been invited to sit on a panel at the New England regional meeting of the American College of Trust and Estate Counsel, a preeminent national organization of trusts and estates lawyers and academics. An expert on the newest Connecticut tax laws, he was confident that he knew the material he was slated to present. But he was a lousy traveler and a nervous speaker. Getting a good night's sleep in a hotel room had never been an easy task. Doing so the night before a big speech had proven effectively impossible. So he was annoyed but not at all surprised when he found himself walking the streets of Boston when he should have been resting comfortably a few floors above.

Jack's sleepless night may have been due in large part to one unfortunate coincidence. The conference hotel was just a few blocks from where he was staying. But Jack had instead elected to book a room at the Van Buren, hoping that he would find a better night's sleep at the quieter hotel a few blocks removed from the Hilton, where the conference attendees were all gathering. It hadn't worked. As fate would have it, Governor Daniel Milbank, the event's keynote speaker, had booked his stay at the Van Buren as well. When Jack had caught sight of the governor and a pair of troopers exiting the lobby yesterday afternoon, his anxiety had spiked. *This was a big conference with a big audience*, he had been reminded at that moment and had since been unable to forget it. Thus the decision to book a hotel off the beaten path had spectacularly backfired, heightening Jack's anxiety rather than mitigating it. A largely sleepless night had been the result.

He rounded the corner of Post Office Square and headed the wrong way down Franklin Street, planning to take one more loop around the block before returning to his hotel. It was nearly six o'clock, and he wasn't due to speak until after lunch. Maybe, just maybe, he could catch some sleep between now and then. If he really drifted off, he could skip the governor's morning address and watch the recording later. That seemed like a reasonable plan. He hoped it would work.

As he neared the hotel, a black sedan lurched to a halt in front of the entrance. Two people, a man and a woman, emerged from the lobby and stepped into the piercing spotlights shining down from the building's facade. The man wheeled a small suitcase to the back of the car, placed it in the trunk, and slammed the lid closed.

The woman went to the driver, who was holding open the rear door of the car. She said something then glanced in Jack's direction before getting into the back seat.

Jack was only about fifty feet away, and he recognized her immediately. His stomach clenched. *Huh? What is she doing here?*

The engine roared back to life. As the car pulled away from the curb, the man stepped back into the spotlights then went back into the hotel.

Kyle Stone hadn't seemed to notice Jack. But Jack had definitely seen him.

Suddenly, everything made sense. And the problem was bigger than he had ever imagined.

Chapter 73

Jack dialed Joe Andrews's cell.

Joe answered on the first ring. He apparently hadn't been sleeping either. "Wow, you're up early. I figured I'd let you sleep a bit."

"I just saw Kyle going into the Van Buren," Jack reported before having to pause to catch his breath.

"Back on duty, I guess."

"He was with Jessica Baldwin."

"*What?*"

"I just saw them." Jack peered up at the windows of the hotel. He turned his back to it and walked a few feet away. "He put her into a car."

"That makes no sense. Kyle was at a bar all night. He had quite the night. Almost punched out some kid from BC and kept trying to get Levine to go back to his hotel room with him. No way he was with Baldwin."

"He wasn't. Baldwin was with *Milbank*. The governor is staying at this hotel."

"Are you sure?"

"Positive."

"Holy shit. Did you get a picture of her leaving?"

"What?"

"A *picture*, like on your phone? Something that backs up your story?"

"My *story*? Joe, I know who I saw."

"I know you do, but we've been through this. They're about to leave my jurisdiction. I'm not the one you need to convince anymore. I'm not sure "Trust me. My buddy Jack saw them" is going to be quite enough to get New Haven to go for a wiretap."

Jack's stomach was in knots. He looked around, trying to find a dis-crete place to vomit. He spotted a promising garbage can about ten paces down the street.

"Go back to your room," Joe said. "Give me some time. I'll call you soon."

"Okay." Jack reached the garbage can just in time to lean over it and empty his morning coffee."

"That didn't sound good. You okay?"

"Yeah," Jack spit into the can and swiped his sleeve across his mouth. "Just perfect."

<hr />

A FEW HOURS LATER, Jack's phone buzzed on the nightstand be-side his bed. He forced himself to respond to the sound, his eyes and body seemingly reacting at half their normal speed. He picked up his cell and slowly lifted it toward his face. The display showed that it was nine thirty. He sat up, noticing happily that he was far less nauseous than he had been a few hours earlier, a faint headache the only linger-ing remnant of his sleep-deprived night and chaotic morning. He an-swered the call. "Hey, Joe."

"How are you doing?"

"Better. I actually got some sleep." Jack ran his tongue around his parched mouth.

"I'm glad. And I've got some good news."

"Thank God." Jack grabbed his water bottle off the nightstand, twisted off the cap, and took a swig.

"We're going to get another shot at this."

"I thought New Haven wouldn't just trust me."

"Oh, they don't," Joe said, laughing. "I had that one right. But fear not. I figured out another solution and called in a chit."

"That's good, right?"

"Yes, if it works out. It's a bit of a longshot, but I say we try it."

"So what's the plan?" Jack took another sip of water then swished it around in his mouth.

"We're still working on the final details, so let's talk once you're back home. We'll have it all figured out by then."

"Okay." It really wasn't. Uncertainty was one of Jack's least favorite things, and Joe was offering up a plateful of it.

"I'll set something up for tomorrow. You free in the morning?"

Jack scrolled though his schedule. He didn't see anything he couldn't move. "Sure. Let's do it. What's the worst that can happen?"

"You don't really want me to answer that, do you?"

Jack's nausea came roaring back. "No, I don't. Not at all."

Chapter 74

Kyle sped west on the Mass Pike in a nondescript SUV, the single-digit license plate—the number one—the sole indicator of the occupant. That important passenger sat in the backseat, flipping through a briefing book, a set of earphones isolating him from Kyle and the rest of the world.

"Excuse me, sir," Kyle said over his shoulder.

The governor uncovered one ear. "Yeah?" he replied without looking up. "What do you need?"

Even in this private space, Kyle had accorded the governor the proper respect. It was always "sir," always "governor," even on poker nights or when it was just the two of them alone in in the car. But the governor too often did not return such courtesy. Sure, when people were watching, Milbank was polite and respectful. But when there was no audience, he rarely gave Kyle his full attention, and his tone was typically informal and dismissive. Perhaps Kyle had been naïve to expect otherwise. He had seen how Milbank treated his own family in private. He really couldn't expect better for himself.

"I have some time coming to me. I could really use a break."

"Okay," Milbank said, still not raising his eyes from his book.

"I'm thinking a few days in Vegas. Maybe I'll leave this weekend? A chance to refill the tank."

"Sure. Duncan can handle things."

Kyle had hoped the governor might protest, even if only slightly.

With the election right around the corner, Milbank should have wanted Kyle to work continuously until that crucial day. The governor should have *needed* him. But Milbank clearly didn't.

Kyle glanced in the rearview mirror. The governor, his headphones back in as he answered a call, couldn't care less about him. Kyle was just a commodity in the governor's life. If he couldn't drive for him, then someone else would. Of course, if Milbank needed something more, Kyle's importance would suddenly grow, at least fleetingly. Milbank would pick up his burner and summon Kyle from wherever he was and whatever he was doing, Kyle's own life be damned. Milbank would bark out an order, and Kyle would come running. That was the way it had always been. That was the way it would always be.

Milbank laughed at whatever the person on the other end of the phone said, lost in his own little world, clueless to the fact that Kyle was even there, that there was another human being in this car. Without Kyle driving, Milbank would be getting nowhere right now. It was a suitable metaphor for Kyle's whole career. But the great governor was oblivious to that, taking for granted the man who was literally responsible for getting him where he needed to go.

I don't need this anymore. Kyle's fury rose as he watched the governor in the mirror. Kyle had gotten all he could hope for out of this relationship. It was time to move on.

When Milbank ended his call, Kyle asked one last question. "You ever stay at the Bellagio in Vegas, sir?"

The governor nodded. "I have. Overpriced. Not sure you want to bother on your salary."

"Maybe I'll splurge." Kyle laughed heartily. "Just this once."

Chapter 75

Jack sat across from Jessica Baldwin, waiting for her to finish looking through the paperwork. He had just completed a rather uneventful status conference on the Heller estate, confirming that all was back on track after Tom's death and would be wrapped up soon. His audit revealed that five million dollars had been misappropriated from the estate, an amount unrecoverable because it had disappeared through a string of offshore banks. But his malpractice carrier had already refunded the amount to the estate. Mrs. Heller would get her full inheritance. CWO would take a reputational hit but not a financial one. They could all move forward.

"Thank you for coming in," the judge said as she tidied the files in front of her. "I'm glad we can put this ugly episode behind us."

As he'd done for the last ten minutes, Jack suppressed the urge to tell the judge what he truly thought of her false courtesy and her smug smiles. Instead, he returned her smile with a fake one of his own. His legs began to quiver as he shut his briefcase and stood it on the floor beside his chair. *Here we go.*

"You know, something still doesn't quite add up," Jack said, struggling to keep his expression neutral and his tone innocent. "I can't figure out why Tom did it. He had plenty of money. He was doing just fine."

"Don't people always want more?" she asked. "Greed is a powerful motive."

"I guess so," he said with a small shrug. "Well, trust me. We'll get to the bottom of it."

"I think you have gotten to the bottom of it." She tapped the file on her desk. "Your client has been made whole. It's time to move on."

Jack shook his head. "I don't know. I can't get myself to just walk away."

"Walk away." She waved a hand in the air. "Let the man rest in peace."

"If only I knew who Kyle was..."

Her head snapped back, and she peered at him intently. "Excuse me?"

"Oh, I was just kind of thinking out loud there." He pretended to wince. "It's nothing, Your Honor." He looked down at the tabletop. "Please forget I said anything."

She frowned and leaned forward in her chair. "What's going on, Attorney Collins?"

"I need to do some more research before I know exactly how to answer that. I just found some materials Tom had hidden away. I think they might point to more illegal activity, I'm sorry to say. Once I know more, I'll certainly disclose it to the court."

"I'm afraid that's not good enough," she snapped. "If you're aware of something improper, I need to hear about it. Now!"

"I'm not trying to withhold anything, Your Honor. Most of the records are encrypted, so we hired someone to work on them. I promise you we will notify the proper authorities as soon as we find anything more." He stood and picked up his briefcase.

"Not so fast, Attorney Collins." She pointed at his chair. Once he was seated again, she asked, "What kind of records are we talking about?"

"A flash drive. It was hidden in his office."

"And you mentioned a name. Kyle, I think you said?"

"Yes, Your Honor. One document wasn't encrypted. That name, Kyle, was mentioned along with some bank account information. The bank account is probably a dead end, but I assure you, we are going to aggressively pursue it. We'll try to figure out who this Kyle is and see where that leads. I promise you, if Tom engaged in any other misconduct, we'll fully disclose it to the court." As he tussled with this tiger, Jack miraculously didn't feel his usual panic. His heartbeat was steady, and his palms remained dry.

Their traditional roles had now reversed. Her eyes were wide with panic. She gasped in a shallow breath through an open mouth. She was no longer in control of this room, far from it.

"No! You need to drop this."

"Believe me, I'd love to ignore all this." His adrenaline now kicking in, Jack reined in his excitement. "But I don't think I can. I have an obligation to the court."

"No, you do not!" Her nostrils flared, and her face reddened. "And you need to think carefully here. What's the upside of digging around in Tom's past? What if he'd been doing this for years? Those estates are all settled. Your insurer would deny any claims hiding behind approved final accounts and the statute of limitations. So nobody gets any money back, but it would be a major embarrassment for your firm. Your reputation will be ruined."

As she spiraled out of control, Jack simply sat silently, just as he had been instructed to do. He avoided looking at his phone for the same reason. *Look anywhere else*, they had told him. *Never at the phone.*

"And what about me?" She pointed at her chest. "How will I look?"

Jack started to reply but held his tongue. *Let her keep going.*

"Maybe we can work together here?" She cocked her head, and one corner of her mouth lifted. "Maybe there's a better way to help us both out?"

"What are you suggesting?" he asked, letting out a bit of rope.

She walked over to her desk and came back with a thick file. "I need a guardian for this estate. Arthur Cromwell. I'm sure you recognize the name."

He nodded. "Of course."

"It's a hundred-thousand-dollar fee."

"A hundred thousand dollars for acting as a guardian? I'm sorry, Judge. Could you explain that?" *A little more rope.* "And what does that have to do with Tom?"

"What are you, a moron? You know the way this works. Take the guardianship. Give me everything Tom left behind and drop it. Just take the fee, and keep your mouth shut."

"So like a trade?"

Her smug smile was back. She clearly thought she was back in control, unaware that she was about to learn a harsher truth. "Yeah, like a trade."

Jack's gut clenched. *Was that enough?* he wondered. He wished he had paid better attention in criminal procedure class back in law school.

Chapter 76

Bill Clayton got into the passenger seat of Kyle's cruiser and slammed the door behind him. "How's my favorite trooper?" the reporter asked.

"Doing just fine, thanks. I'm wrapping some things up and then flying off to Vegas for a little R and R."

"What did they do to piss you off?" Clayton chuckled. "Must have been good."

Kyle merely laughed. *Wouldn't you like to know?* He passed Clayton the promised envelope. "There are some text messages in there. They should be enough to convince you."

"How long has it been going on?" Clayton asked, pulling out his notebook.

"Years. From the moment she was on the bench."

Clayton's eyes widened as he scribbled something down on a fresh page.

"Will you put anything on the record?"

Kyle scoffed. "No way."

"Unnamed member of the Governor's staff?"

"I'm not really on his staff."

Clayton shrugged. "It's close enough."

"Yeah, sure."

Clayton positioned his pencil over his notebook. "What's the comment?"

"What's my comment?"

"Yeah, what does the unnamed staffer have to stay?"

Kyle rubbed his chin. He worked through a few permutations in his head "It has been an affair and a business arrangement." He paused, mentally sharpening his next line. "The governor and the judge are a power couple who will stop at nothing to get what they want."

"Ouch!" Clayton said, still writing. "That will hurt."

Kyle smiled. *They deserved it. Every bit of it.*

"Anything else?" the reporter asked.

"There's a name and phone number in there." Kyle pointed at the envelope on Clayton's lap. "He's a limo driver in Boston. Good guy. He'll confirm a rendezvous at the Van Buren."

Clayton nodded. "So, what do you want?"

In all their years together, Kyle had never given Clayton anything nearly this big, the first clear path in pursuit of what would turn out to be an epic scandal. With this information, Clayton would bring down a judge and a governor. He would put his small Connecticut newspaper up there with the *Washington Post* and *New York Times*. He might even win another Pulitzer, sticking his thumb in the eyes of his old friends at the *Hartford Courant* in the process. The contents of that envelope were priceless. Whatever Kyle asked for, Clayton was likely prepared to give.

Kyle thought about all that Jessica Baldwin had cost him: the arrest, the scandal, the lost opportunities, and the years she'd manipulated and lied to him, denying him the chance to know the truth about his father, denying him the chance to properly say goodbye. No money or flattering publicity would make that whole. But whatever pain he could bring her would help soothe the old wound, help settle the score.

His heart full of malice, thinking of nothing other than revenge, Kyle grinned. "Believe it or not, I want absolutely nothing in return."

Chapter 77

Jack's watch finally buzzed on his wrist. He glanced down and surreptitiously read the message.

That's probably enough. But try to get more. Go for broke.

Jack patted the Cromwell folder. "So is this all there is?"

"Excuse me?"

"I mean Kyle and Tom took *millions*. A hundred grand is nice, but there's got to be more."

The judge straightened. "I have no idea what you're talking about," she said, her voice quaking.

"Look, Judge Baldwin, I was being a bit coy before. In truth, I've almost figured it all out. I know about Kyle Stone, your old high school friend."

Her eyes narrowed. "Where are you going with this?"

"And I know about you and the governor. So is it the three of you? Is that the whole operation?"

"Are you trying to *extort* me?"

"Absolutely not," Jack said slowly and clearly. "You're the one who offered a trade. That was *your* idea. I'm just asking if maybe you want to make a larger trade."

"You know what?" She jumped to her feet. "I'm done."

His heart fell. She'd definitely incriminated herself, but the evidence was far from ironclad.

"I'm not going to trade." She jabbed her finger toward his face. "But I'm going to give you a warning. Kyle is smart and ruthless. You don't want to cross him, and by extension, you don't want to cross me. Now, as best I can tell, you just came in here and tried to extort me with some spurious allegations."

Jack stood and gave her an incredulous look. "You're going to deny that *you* just tried to bribe *me*?"

"My word against yours. And I'll win. You know why? Because I've got friends you can't even dream of. I have the state police. I have the fucking *governor*. You do not want to mess with them or with me. So take that Cromwell matter as my gift, and keep your mouth shut. You hear me?"

Jack's whole body flushed, blood pounding through his veins. This was not fear. This was triumph. "Keep my mouth shut or what?" he asked, setting her up for another self-inflicted blow.

"Or Kyle Stone will shut it for you."

"Is that a threat?"

"Oh, it's so much more than that."

His wrist buzzed. He looked down at the screen and smiled.

On our way.

Jack had time to ask one final question. "Who told you I was having a girl?"

"Huh?"

"One day, you mentioned it after a hearing. You talked about my wife being pregnant, about our future *daughter*."

"I don't know. One of the clerks mentioned it, I think." She shrugged. "Why should I remember that?"

"Nobody mentioned it," Jack said as he backed toward the door. "Nobody *knew* it. Amanda and I had kept that private, even from our parents."

Baldwin leaned toward Jack, her arms crossed against her chest, her nostrils flaring. "I'm not sure what you're trying to get at."

"You tapped Tom's phone. And you tapped mine too. And that's why you all think I'm done with the FBI. That's why you think they've walked away from this whole case. But they haven't. Far from it."

Jack could hear a growing commotion in the lobby—a few raised voices, punctuated by some sharp shouts. *They must be having some fun, putting on a good show.*

"What is going on out there?" Jessica yelled toward the closed courtroom door.

As the door flung open, she got her answer. A man stormed across the threshold, his floppy windbreaker bearing an embroidered FBI shield. A second badge dangled from a lanyard around his neck. Three other agents pushed in behind him, an ample show of force.

"Special Agent Bob Masterson!" the first man bellowed. "FBI."

Jessica's face turned a sickly shade of white. She spun toward Jack, her narrow eyes full of contempt. "Do you know what you've done?"

Agent Masterson moved between the judge and Jack. "Judge Baldwin, please place your hands behind your back. I'm going to read you your Miranda rights and then place you under arrest."

Some shocked clerks looked on through the doorway, making the judge's humiliation nearly complete.

"You're going to cuff me?" she scoffed.

"Yes, ma'am," he replied calmly.

Another agent removed the FBI cell phone from the table and handed Jack his own phone. "Nice work," he said as he slipped the listening device into his pocket. "We were dying with laughter out in the van. You really nailed her at the end."

Chapter 78

Kyle's burner phone buzzed as it vibrated on the dashboard. "Yeah," he answered.

"Bad news, bro," Mike Daly said. "They busted Baldwin."

"What?" Kyle jerked the wheel and nearly clipped the car in the next lane. "Hang on." He flipped on his emergency lights, and the red and blue beacons cleared a path for him as he swerved onto the shoulder. *Busted?* Who busted her?"

"Just heard it from one of my buds in New Haven. Feds picked her up at her courthouse. Made a big show of it. At least three agents."

"New Haven guys? Why the hell didn't you know this was coming?"

"Good question. There was something weird going on. Arresting guy came up from New York."

New York? What the hell? "You talked to Sanchez and Watson?"

"Yeah, I talked to all my boys over there. Came out of nowhere. Nobody even knew she was under surveillance."

She wasn't. Kyle had seen the texts himself.

"And here's something," Daly added. "Tom's law partner, this guy Collins, was there when Baldwin got busted. He might have been the snitch."

"Where is she now?" Kyle's shirt was starting to stick to his back. He tugged the front away from his chest to get some air flowing.

"On her way to New Haven."

"Crap." Kyle knew what would happen next. They would question her then quickly offer her a deal. She could afford to lawyer up and stay silent. If he had any luck at all, she would do exactly that, at least for a little while. Hopefully, he had enough time to get away.

He had already made his choice to leave. But the judge's arrest forced the timeline. If he disappeared now, he'd look guilty as hell. But sticking around was unthinkable. Jessica couldn't be trusted. His dear childhood friend would once again throw him under the bus to save her own skin. He didn't have a good option, but leaving was clearly better than staying.

"Okay, man, I'm going dark here," he said. "If anyone asks, I'm in Vegas. Say I mentioned the Bellagio. Act like you're ratting me out."

"Got it. You need me to clean anything up?"

Kyle thought about it. Right now, they would have him on all the financial stuff. There was nothing to tie either him or Daly to Tom's murder, which Baldwin still thought was just an overdose. Or so she had said. He wasn't quite sure if she had been playing coy. He also didn't know if she knew about that part of the plot. Either way, he wasn't about to take any chances.

"Yeah," Kyle said. "The lawyer? Collins? Find out what he knows. Make sure he has no clue who I am and doesn't know about your little visit with his partner."

"I got it."

"Good. Thanks."

"And then?"

Kyle parroted one of Daniel Milbank's favorite lines. "Do whatever you need to do."

Kyle ended the call, pulled off the shoulder, and merged back into traffic. Racing home, he mentally traced the path he would take to the hunting cabin to make his escape to the blue skies of Colorado. The moment had come. It was time to go, time to leave them all behind. He only hoped it wasn't too late.

Chapter 79

Jessica Baldwin sat in a windowless room, fiddling with the splintered edge of the warped wooden table. She stared at the large mirror mounted on the wall in front of her and wondered who was staring back.

Her lawyer sat at her side, his hand resting on her arm, a reassuring gesture that provided little solace. While occasionally whispering some encouraging sentiment in her ear, the thirty-year veteran of the Connecticut bar knew how to tally the score. At every turn, he had made it clear just how bad her situation was. She had no way of getting out of this. Exoneration was impossible.

Her only hope, and one that would merely get her a lighter sentence, was to make the police's work easier and to be the first to do so. "The first deal would be the best one," he had told her. "Take it before someone else does."

The lawyer in her knew he had given her sage advice. Without her help, the FBI would need only a few days to follow the trail to Danny Milbank. But if she assisted, they would get to the governor in minutes. Saving them that time could slice years off her own prison sentence. Yet, her decision was far from made.

She stood and started pacing the length of the room, trying to ignore the recording equipment sitting on top of the dinged table and the pen lying beside it. She stopped behind her chair and leaned against it, eyeing the menacing pen. *Could she be the one to sign Danny's death warrant? Did she have that in her?*

Her stomach tensed as the door creaked open. Agent Masterson lumbered into the room, carrying a folder in one of his meaty hands. Someone new was with him this time. The second guy had a better haircut, and his suit was properly tailored. He was obviously higher up in the food chain of the FBI. When he introduced himself as Special Agent in Charge Steven Alvarez, she wasn't surprised.

Alvarez gestured at the table, and Jessica pulled out her chair and sat beside her lawyer again. Masterson sat across from her while Alvarez took the seat next to him.

Alvarez turned on the recorder and reviewed the terms of the offer. "It's not immunity," he said. "It's not even a formal cooperation agreement. I want to make that clear. But the FBI will urge your cooperation to be taken into account during sentencing. You have my word on that, but it's all we can offer."

Her lawyer leaned over and whispered in her ear. "Take it. We've got no leverage. It's all you can hope for."

She closed her eyes and pictured Danny's face as he slept beside her at the Van Buren. She heard his gentle breathing. She felt her chest pressed against the warmth of his body. As imperfect as they both were, there was something undeniable about what they had, what they still had. The two of them against the world. An unstoppable team.

This wasn't an ending she'd ever pictured. This wasn't the ending they deserved. Her nose burned as a single tear fought past the will of her pride and streamed down her cheek. She sniffled. Her attorney pressed a tissue into her hand.

"Judge Baldwin," Alvarez said, "are you ready to make a statement?"

She swiped at her eyes with the Kleenex. *What would Danny do if he were in her spot?* She was certain of the answer. He was ruthless and calculating. He would turn on Kyle. He would give up his entire inner circle. She had seen him plot. She had seen him strike. But he had never turned on her. Never once. And he never would.

"No," she replied.

Alvarez raised one eyebrow. "Excuse me?"

She shook her head. "I will not make a statement." The reassuring hand on her arm now encircled it.

"Can you give us a minute?" her lawyer asked.

"Sure." Alvarez huffed as he turned off the recorder. "But let's keep moving. This deal won't last much longer."

Chapter 80

Kyle had a row to himself on the nearly empty aircraft, the last flight of the day to Las Vegas. He would be in the air less than six hours. Once in Vegas, he would hop a bus back toward Denver and stay in the city a couple of nights before making his way to the cabin. The trip would be long, but his circuitous path would be difficult to follow, especially given the ample head start provided by the fake driver's license he'd used to whisk through security at JFK.

Even so, taking this flight was a gamble, albeit a calculated one. Travel by car or bus would have been safer but slower. *Too slow.* There was no way he could work his way across the country once he was flagged as a wanted fugitive. There was no way to outrun the hurricane of pursuers that Jessica would soon unleash. But an airplane could move him safely away from the storm, getting him two thousand miles away before anyone started looking for him. Once they finally picked up the chase, they would find his flight record and spot his face on security footage. Milbank would remember the comment about the Bellagio. Daly would drop the same clue with fake reluctance. All of those breadcrumbs would send them on a clear trail toward Vegas while Kyle slipped back toward Granby and disappeared.

This was the only way to slip the noose. *But first, this plane needed to get off the ground.*

He nonchalantly flipped through a magazine and avoided making eye contact with the flight attendant as she worked her way up and down the aisle. He tracked her movement with his ears alone, following her soft footsteps as she moved toward the rear of the plane, her cheerful voice engaging with someone every few rows. And most of all, he listened to the sound of overhead bins shutting in her wake. *Click.* One step closer to the runway. *Click.* Another step closer.

He looked out the window to confirm that the baggage cart had moved away from the plane. Movement inside the cabin was settling down, the empty seats around him looking like they would remain that way. But he still hadn't heard the sound he was waiting for, that of the cabin door slamming shut.

A chime sounded, and the flight attendant shuffled quickly toward the front of the plane. "Ladies and gentlemen," she announced, "please take your seats. At this time, we need everyone to take their seats." She seemed slightly out of breath.

It's fine, he told himself.

The chime sounded again. Out of the corner of his eye, Kyle saw a different flight attendant pass his row as she hustled from the front of the plane. He peeked over his shoulder. She was standing in the aisle just two rows behind his. A moment later, he checked again. A male steward had appeared behind her.

His stomach grew heavy. The door still hadn't closed. He tucked the magazine in the seatback pocket and turned to face the aisle. If they were coming for him, he would have no place to run.

The plane grew eerily quiet as the movement inside ground to a halt. Moments later, he heard the rushing footfalls he had at first been dreading and then anticipating. Two agents in full tactical gear bolted from the first-class section. A couple of passengers shrieked while the rest just murmured. The flight attendants stayed fixed at their posts, their eyes now locked on Kyle.

Kyle unfastened his seatbelt as the agents descended upon him. He raised his hands high, making certain they remained in full view.

"Kyle Stone," the first agent said as he reached Kyle's row, "come with us, please."

Kyle slipped out of his seat, keeping his hands where the agents could see them.

It was over.

Chapter 81

Jack sat back on the sofa, a beer in one hand and the remote control in the other.

"What's your pleasure?" he asked his wife, who had flopped onto the far cushion.

She put her feet up on his lap. "The Yankees game is fine," she said as she nestled deeper into the cushions, sliding back and forth a few times before eventually settling into place.

"I'm glad to do a movie."

"Nah, I'm going to fall asleep anyway. You should watch the game."

If either of them slept tonight, it would be a miracle. Despite the beer's calming effects, he was filled with adrenaline, a new surge added by each of Joe's text messages: *Baldwin is in custody. They caught Kyle. The governor is next.*

Brick by brick, the corrupt tower was being knocked to the ground. Jack wouldn't sleep until it was all done.

As the Yankees trotted onto the field, he looked over at his wife. Her eyes were already closed. She rested one hand on her growing belly, which rose and fell with every breath. This was what it was all about. This was worth all the struggles.

He felt his own eyes grow heavy as the Royals' third baseman stepped into the batter's box. Jack peered at the baby monitor on the end table. His son was fast asleep, a stuffed sheep standing guard beside his head.

All was quiet. His eyelids drooped more every second as he tried to focus on the screen. Finally, he let them close.

Chapter 82

Daniel Milbank sat on a leather sofa in his Greenwich living room, his feet firmly on the floor as he leaned forward on the edge of the cushion. In the chairs across from him sat two of his most senior aides, their glum faces telling the tale. They were in serious trouble.

Despite the late hour, Milbank was wide awake, sleep not even on his radar and likely to be impossible. He was freshly showered and shaved, ready at a moment's notice to swap out the sweatshirt and jogging pants he was wearing for the crisp white shirt and navy suit hanging on his closet doorknob.

At the other end of the room, one of Milbank's attorneys was pacing a groove in the ornate oriental carpet. The lawyer grimaced as he pressed a headphone deeper into his ear. "That's ridiculous!" He shook his head wildly. "Just a publicity stunt." The red-faced man grimaced. "Who the hell over there is in charge of this thing? There's no reason to be turning us down. It's a damn circus."

A *circus*? Milbank's gut tensed. The lawyer was offering what he had cast as a pretty simple deal. Milbank would voluntarily appear at the New Haven FBI office, give a statement, and answer questions. No need for a warrant. No need for a public scene. He would do it all *quietly*. But the FBI apparently had a different plan.

"Oh, give me a break." His lawyer groaned and his shoulders dropped. "When?"

The simple question sent a shiver up Milbank's spine.

"This is beyond the pale," the attorney said. "You are just trying to humiliate him."

Milbank felt the urge to vomit. Amid the chaos in the living room, he heard another set of agitated voices coming from the foyer.

His wife screamed. Milbank jumped up and ran toward the front door. She was standing on the marble floor, a small suitcase tucked behind her and a state trooper blocking her path.

"Mrs. Milbank," the trooper said, "we really need to stay inside for now."

"You need to stand aside." She jabbed a finger at him. "Now!"

The trooper turned to the governor. "Sir, Mrs. Milbank wants to leave. I've tried to explain to her that it's not a good idea."

The governor stepped up beside his wife and placed a hand on her shoulder. "Let's go back upstairs," he said calmly, smiling at the trooper as he dug his fingernails into his wife's flesh.

Whenever Milbank next stepped through that front door, she would be by his side, her fingers interlaced with his, her support unwavering. She'd been cast in the part of the loyal, loving wife, whether she had any desire to play that role or not. She'd been told that. *Explicitly.* "Come on," he said, tugging gently on her shoulder as she struggled to slip away.

"Please open the door," she said to the trooper, her tone clinical as she simply ignored her husband's presence, "unless you want a false imprisonment charge."

The trooper looked at the governor with wide eyes.

Milbank leaned toward his wife and snarled in her ear, "You walk out on me now, and you're done for. I'll tie you up in court for years. You won't get a penny."

She laughed as she dipped her shoulder and slipped from his grip. "Oh, Danny, you have so many bigger problems to deal with right now. I'm really the least of your worries."

"Get upstairs!" he ordered, completely sick of playing her game.

She motioned for the trooper to open the front door. This time, he complied.

She smirked. "Good luck, Danny."

"What the hell are you doing?" Milbank snapped at the trooper. "I'm the goddammed governor."

"Not much longer," his wife taunted as she stepped into the night.

Chapter 83

Jack's eyes snapped open. At first, he wasn't sure what had woken him. A noise came from the kitchen, the sound of shattering glass. He bolted upright, and the room swirled around him. His ears started pounding.

More glass broke, followed by a crashing noise. Heavy footsteps clapped on the kitchen floor.

Amanda sat up beside him, her eyes wide. "What's going on?"

"Grab Nate," Jack whispered.

She swung her feet to the floor. Her mouth fell open.

He helped her from the sofa. "Go."

As Amanda fled down the hall toward the bedrooms, Jack raced in the opposite direction, away from his loved ones and toward the sound of danger.

"Who's there?" he yelled as he crossed into the kitchen, trying to attract attention to himself and away from his wife. "What do you want?"

A man in black stood beside the refrigerator. He raised his right hand and pointed a gun directly at Jack's chest.

"Hello, Jack." The man pushed Jack backward into the living room. "We've got some stuff to talk about."

Chapter 84

Daniel Milbank stepped back into the living room as his lawyer reached what seemed to be the end of the road with the FBI.

"Yeah, you too," the lawyer snapped into his phone. "Thanks for *nothing*." He disconnected the call and sighed. "I'm sorry, Governor. They won't agree. I got an across-the-board 'No deal.'"

"What?" Milbank's stomach dropped as a sense of powerlessness overtook him. His lawyer had said this would be easy. He'd said he would make it happen. He'd lied.

"They want a public arrest, a spectacle."

Milbank slashed his hands in the air. "No way. No way in hell!"

"Then we have to give them something, sir. We need a bargaining chip. You have to give them Judge Baldwin."

"What if I give them Kyle?"

The lawyer shook his head. "No, sir. Not good enough."

"What if we find that guy who killed the lawyer and offer him up? He's one of Daly's thugs. I'm sure we can hunt him down."

The lawyer again shook his head. "I'm sorry, sir. That won't do it. It's you and Judge Baldwin they want. Nobody else matters."

Milbank collapsed onto the sofa. He'd loved Jessica since the day he met her. He could still picture the first time he'd spotted her across the room, the silky brown hair, her dimples when she smiled. Without her, he would never be where he was today. He wouldn't be governor. But then again, he'd also never be in this peril. She was the one who was supposed to protect him. She was the one who should have ensured their plan was never detected. *She* had failed. *She* had slipped up. It was only a matter of time before the FBI figured out everything. He shouldn't have to take the fall for both of them.

Milbank straightened and sat forward. "I'll do it. Call them back."

A minute later, his lawyer was back on the phone. "He's willing to give you Baldwin. He'll tell you everything, including his own role. We just want a private meeting. No agents storming the house. No public display." The lawyer held up a finger toward Milbank then smiled. He placed a hand over the phone. "He's running it up the line. This might just work."

Milbank stared at his shoes. He had done what he needed to do, he tried to reassure himself. It wasn't pretty. But politics never was.

Chapter 85

Agent Alvarez came back into the room, a phone pressed against his ear. He snapped his fingers to get Jessica's attention then pointed at the phone. "Give it to me one more time," he told the person on the line.

He tapped the screen, putting the call on speaker, then turned the phone toward Jessica.

"The governor will give you Baldwin," a voice said. "He'll give you everything."

"How soon is he ready to come in?" Sanchez asked.

"Whenever you want him. As long as we do it quietly."

"I'll get right back to you." Alvarez ended the call and slipped the phone into his jacket pocket. "That was Milbank's lawyer."

Jessica nodded, eyes down. A tear trickled down her cheek.

He walked over to the table, picked up the pen, and began twirling it between his fingers. "My offer to you is still on the table. Do I have your consent to turn on the recorder?"

"Yes," Jessica said before her lawyer could even chime in. Her tears were now impossible to contain. She wiped a sleeve across her face, leaving a trail of tears and makeup on the pricey wool.

Alvarez hit the record button. He named all the parties present and gave the date and time. "Jessica Baldwin, do you intend to waive your rights against self-incrimination and make a statement?"

"Yes," she said, sniffling.

"And is this statement being made voluntarily, of your own free will?"

"Yes." She found the question ironic. There was nothing voluntary about anything she was doing. It simply beat the alternative.

The agent went through a series of questions, the recorder capturing their every word. He asked her about Heller, the Valkenburgh estate, the money, Kyle, and the offshore accounts. Finally, he asked her the only question they probably really cared about.

"Was the governor of Connecticut, Daniel Milbank, involved in this conspiracy to embezzle from the estate of Samuel Heller?"

She felt a flutter in her chest as liquid flowed from her eyes and nose. Her toes were on the edge of the precipice. She looked at her lawyer, who nodded back at her.

She swallowed hard and closed her eyes. What a wonderful couple they could've been... if only. But fate had not been kind to them. And Danny had never quite loved her the way that she loved him. He had never foreseen the future that she had always dreamed of. In the end, it had come down to everyone for themselves. So, she tightened her grip upon the dagger in her hand and thrust it into his heart.

"Yes," she said delivering the fatal blow. "Daniel Milbank was in charge of everything. It was all his idea."

Chapter 86

Jack back-pedaled as the man pressed forward into the living room. Through the wall behind him, he heard a faint clunking noise he pegged as Nate's window blinds flapping against the open window. Jack's pulse slowed as he pictured Amanda and Nate slipping out the nursery window and heading to safety.

Jack's thoughts then turned to his own escape. This was no random break-in. The guy had called Jack by name. He had to be one of Kyle's cronies. But Jack couldn't imagine why Kyle would send someone after him. The FBI was already picking the others off one by one. Kyle should be running for the hills.

Then it dawned on him. The intruder doesn't know.

"The FBI will be here any minute," Jack said, not certain if he was bluffing or not.

The man smiled, tilting an ear toward Jack and revealing an earpiece. "No they won't," he said with a confidence that sent a chill down Jack's spine. "They're always a step behind. Just like with your buddy Tom."

Jack's fear disappeared as anger and adrenaline took over. He stared down Tom's killer. "So you're the one who messed up with the watch."

The man's eyes sharpened. "What are you talking about?"

"You're the one who took them all down. Milbank, Judge Baldwin, and Kyle Stone. Do you want to know how?" he asked, hopefully buying time.

The man had flinched a little with each name Jack rattled off, the gun lowering slightly. He snarled. "You better explain now and fast."

"Remember the watch? The one you planted on Tom? You put it on the *wrong* wrist. Tom was a lefty. He always wore his watch on the right."

"You're full of shit."

"Nope." Jack shook his head. "And now the FBI is arresting people, one by one. Look at my texts," he offered, holding his phone up. "You should run while you can."

"You should shut your damn mouth," the man snarled as he slapped the phone from Jack's hand. It tumbled to the floor as the man leaned menacingly toward Jack's face.

Across the room, Amanda's voice boomed. "The FBI is on their way."

The sound of a passing car punctuated her words. She was on the street, Jack realized, baby monitor in hand. *Brilliant.*

The man looked momentarily disoriented as he tried to pinpoint the source of the new voice. He pivoted away from Jack, the gun sliding sideways as he turned.

Jack jumped at the opportunity. He lurched toward the bookcase. In one fluid motion, he grabbed the old bat leaning against it and swung it forward, aiming at the base of the man's skull. The blow connected with a sickening crack. The man crumpled like a puppet whose strings had been cut. The gun flew from his hand as his face hit the arm of the sofa before he flattened onto the rug.

Jack jumped on his back and grabbed the monitor off the table. "He's down! Get help."

The words were scarcely out of his mouth when Jack heard footsteps crunching across the broken glass in the kitchen. His neighbor, a former Marine, bounded into the living room and piled on the assailant's back.

The Marine took off his belt and jerry-rigged a pair of handcuffs, lashing the downed man's wrists together. "I got this," he said, his tone making clear that he had handled far tougher foes.

Jack stepped away and slid to the floor. He placed his hands on his pounding temples as he gasped for air.

Amanda raced into the room, face wet with tears and Nate perched safely on her right hip. She knelt beside Jack. "Are you okay?"

"Yeah," Jack gasped. "I'm fine."

The man on the floor growled as he came back toward consciousness. He struggled against the weight on his back.

"You're not going anywhere, buddy," the Marine said.

The wail of a siren sounded in the distance. The undulating wail grew louder. A second one joined in, then another, creating a cacophony of yelps and whoops clearly heading their way.

Minutes later, police trooped into the house, cuffed the intruder, and led him away. The Marine made his exit with a patrolman. Amanda settled Nate back in his crib. Jack sat alone at the kitchen table as the remaining cops surveyed the scene.

A young officer entered the kitchen, holding a baseball bat in a gloved hand. "Is this yours?" he asked.

"Yes," Jack replied.

"It's a family heirloom," Amanda added as she stepped into the room.

"Looks like it came in handy," the cop said.

"Oh yeah, we love that thing," Amanda replied, running her fingers playfully through Jack's hair. "It's from Bat Day, you know."

Chapter 87

Jack stood at the living-room window, hoping a large cup of coffee would undo the effects of a long, sleepless night. The blinds were all shut tightly, shielding his tired eyes from the early-morning sunlight. He peeked through two slats and was reassured by the sight of a Stamford police car parked in front of his house. He turned toward the muffled sound of slippers on carpet.

Amanda shuffled over to stand beside him and wrapped her arm around his shoulders. "You doing okay?"

"I'm hanging in there." *Barely*. "I'll be better when all this is over."

"That makes two of us."

He checked his watch. It was almost nine. Showtime according to Joe.

He found the remote control and waved it in the air. "Shall we?"

"Go for it." She sat on the couch.

He dropped down beside her and turned on the television. After a few minutes, the news came on. The leading story was the scandal involving the governor. The camera cut from the anchor to show the chaos unfolding in front of Governor Daniel Milbank's Old Greenwich home. A panoramic shot filled the screen, centered on the thin yellow line of police tape struggling to hold back a wall of reporters. Flashing red and blue lights bounced off the white clapboard siding of the colonial. Interspersed among the live shots from Old Greenwich were stills and video clips from the governor's years in office. All of it, per the reporter, was about to come to a crashing end.

Amanda took Jack's hand as the Milbanks' front door opened. Two men toting briefcases walked out of the house. Next, the governor, impeccably dressed in a navy suit and crisp white shirt, emerged into the morning light. The scene grew louder as the crowd began shouting. The reporter's cadence quickened as she struggled to be heard over the growing frenzy.

Milbank walked slowly down the front steps amid a cadre of state troopers. He looked as carefree as ever. He held his head high as he waved at the gathering of people, acting as though he was leaving a political campaign site, just another stroll to the car, just another day at the office.

It was anything but.

The reporter narrated breathlessly, talking of indictments and prison terms as the governor's group headed down the front walkway and toward a waiting car.

The camera panned away from the governor and toward those gathered beyond the police tape. A few frenzied supporters demonstrated their unyielding adoration by waving campaign signs or jumping up and down as if trying to attract the governor's eye. Most just watched in what looked to be horrified disbelief or stunned silence, their phones held high to capture the historic moment.

Milbank reached the car, a nondescript silver sedan with its rear door propped open. The governor turned back to the crowd, generating a cascade of applause punctuated by scattered boos. He raised his arms above his head, two fists held high in a final show of strength for the faithful. A final goodbye.

The governor slipped into the car and disappeared from view. The door closed, and the troopers dispersed.

Minutes later, a line of red and blue lights flowed out of the driveway and snaked onto the street, the lone silver sedan sandwiched in the middle. A different camera captured them driving by then panned to follow the line of cars as it moved away.

The reporter continued to narrate the scene as the red and blue lights grew fainter and fainter. Milbank's car slowly faded into the morning light.

Then finally, he was gone.

Epilogue

Five months later...

Jack sat on a bench at the edge of the small slate patio, basking in the sunshine of an unusually warm March morning. Just beyond the flagstones, Nate ran back and forth across the lawn, occasionally pausing to poke at one of the weeds shooting up amid the grass.

"How's everything going with my boys?" Amanda asked as she pushed a stroller around the side of the house.

"We're having a great time back here." Jack unbuckled his daughter from the stroller and lifted her, gently cradling her head as he did so.

"She didn't want to sleep today," Amanda reported. "So we just watched the ducks."

"No nap today, Emily?" Jack asked his daughter as he held her face playfully close to his.

In the distance, the doorbell rang, the chime barely reaching their ears.

"You expecting someone?" he asked.

"Maybe your mother? I thought she said after lunch though."

"She's probably early. I'll get it."

Jack held Emily against his chest as he walked across the patio and through the house. When he passed the front windows, he saw a state police car parked at the curb and a black SUV in his driveway. When his gaze dropped to the license plate, his throat went dry. He rued his decision to skip his morning shower and toss on a ratty sweatshirt.

He smoothed his hair with his free hand then opened the front door. A woman stood on the front porch with a state trooper by her side.

"Governor Williams," Jack said, "it's an honor."

She extended a hand, which Jack awkwardly shook with his left so he could keep a firm grip on Emily.

"Would you like to come in?" Jack asked.

She nodded. "Just for a minute."

Nate came careening through the house, squealing with abandon as he collided with Jack and wrapped himself around his legs.

"My son, Nate," Jack said, introducing the young man, now rolling on the floor, to the state's highest elected official.

Amanda ran into the room, repeating a goofy rendition of "Mama's gonna get you" several times as she approached. She stopped when she saw the guest standing in her foyer.

"My wife, Amanda," Jack said with pride.

Amanda, her unwashed hair flopping out of a loose ponytail, shook the governor's hand then lifted Emily out of Jack's arms.

"Your children are adorable," the governor said, clearly unfazed by the chaos. "My twins are seven now. They grow up quickly. And listen, I'm so sorry to interrupt a Saturday, but I was in the neighborhood."

"You're not interrupting at all," Amanda said. "Can I offer you something to drink?"

"No, thank you. I just came from a breakfast and I'm on my way to a lunch, so I'm pretty well fed." She chuckled then turned toward Jack and raised an eyebrow. "I really just came to ask a question. Have you made up your mind?"

She was certainly persistent. Jack had hemmed and hawed with her staffers. He had promised to think about it and said he'd get back to them soon. For her part, Amanda had urged him to say yes, as had his supportive law partners. But Jack still wasn't sure. It was something he had never before considered. It would be a massive change. And so, he had been dodging the question.

The dodging had just come to an end.

"I'm sure I don't need to tell you, but this opportunity might never come again," the governor pressed. "Under the new statute, I can fill the vacancy by appointment. It would be the chance of a lifetime for you, and a major political victory for me. No better way to turn the page."

Jack was taken by her candor. From the moment he first saw her, back when she was Attorney General, he had been impressed with Alicia Williams. She told it like it was at every turn and was willing to lay bare her own political considerations. Her transparency marked a refreshing change from the style of her predecessor.

Amanda stepped beside Jack and subtly poked him in the ribs. He looked over to see her nodding while she gently moved Emily's head up and down as well.

He took a deep breath. He couldn't say no. If that had ever been an option, it was no longer. "Yes, Governor." He gave her a broad smile. "I'd be honored."

Amanda wrapped her free arm around him and kissed him on the cheek. Emily cooed in his ear.

The governor extended her hand. "Congratulations, Judge Collins," she said as her grip tightened. "I'll have my staff call you to work out announcement details." She grinned. "Try to return their calls this time."

"I will, Governor. I promise."

After another exchange of handshakes, the governor was back on the porch. "You know," she said looking up at their home, "I really love this house. It's wonderful to see a classic preserved like this."

"Thank you," Jack said. "We are very happy here."

"I'll bet. It's so cozy. What a lovely place to raise a family." She walked out to her car.

Amanda grabbed Jack's hand, wrapping her fingers around his. They watched as the SUV backed out of the driveway then drove off into the morning light.

"So, Judge Collins," Amanda said as she tousled his hair, "you might want to grab a shower. There's no telling who might show up next."

Acknowledgments

Writing a second novel proved even more challenging than the first, the fear of a sophomore slump hanging over my head and my computer keyboard. I'm grateful to all those readers who sent such kind encouragement along the way from places near and far. I hope you enjoy this work even more than you did book one.

A number of published authors continue to be so kind to this relative newbie. Thank you, Ian Ayres, Robert Bailey, John Dobbyn, James Grippando, Brad Meltzer, Sheryn MacMunn, and Jonathan Putnam for taking time away from your own writing to guide me with mine.

I'm also thankful for the dear friends who volunteered to read drafts and offer sage advice on my early drafts. Thank you, Andrea Cohen, Jennifer Warner Cooper, Alison Creed, John Stack, and Michele Walters for your friendship and your generosity. In a class by herself among these beta readers is my wife, Alexandra, a lawyer, school librarian, and avid reader whose expertise I would be lost without.

For technical advice, thank you to law student and EMT Michael Coudert and a cadre of other experts—including a criminal defense lawyer, an FBI agent, and a former Assistant United States Attorney—all of whom provided useful general information and asked not to be identified herein.

For all the amazing editorial work and assistance behind the scenes, thank you to Lynn McNamee, Angie Gallion, Erica Lucke Dean, and everyone at Red Adept Publishing. Thank you also to my mentor, Jennifer Klepper, and my amazing fellow authors at Red Adept for all the support and guidance.

I owe so much to my superagent, Liza Fleissig, as well as to Ginger Harris-Dontzin and the rest of the team at the Liza Royce Agency.

This book, and its author, are much the better due to Liza's vision, enthusiasm, and unrelenting efforts on our behalf. And speaking of the world's best literary agency, thank you also to my new family at LRA, the amazing friends and fellow authors who are an endless source of advice, good humor, and inspiration.

As this book went through the editorial process, I lost a wonderful friend, Victor Simonte. His name is honored in the pages of this book, and his memory is held dear by all who knew and loved him.

About the Author

Jeff Cooper is a law professor, lawyer, former Presidential candidate, and published author of both fiction and nonfiction. A graduate of Harvard College, Yale Law School and New York University School of Law, he spent much of his career working in the law firms and trust banks fictionalized in his novels.

His nonfiction writing has been published in Law Journals across the country, excerpted in prominent legal casebooks and treatises, and reprinted both in the U.S. and abroad. His debut novel was a finalist for The Daphne du Maurier Award for Excellence in Mystery/Suspense.

Jeff was born and raised in New York and now lives in Greenwich, Connecticut, where he has served as an elected member of the Representative Town Meeting, a Justice of the Peace and a Director of several non-profit organizations. He is married with three children. When he's not teaching or writing, he can be found on the golf course.

Read more at www.jeffcooperauthor.com.

About the Publisher

Dear Reader,

We hope you enjoyed this book. Please consider leaving a review on your favorite book site.

Visit https://RedAdeptPublishing.com to see our entire catalogue.

Check out our app for short stories, articles, and interviews. You'll also be notified of future releases and special sales.

Printed in Great Britain
by Amazon

56929760R00148